PRETTY

IN PREACH

HIS WEAPON HER BLESSING

A Novel by

Destiny

To submit a manuscript for our review,

email us at

submissions@majorkeypublishing.com

To my late Grampa,

I hope you're proud of me

Chapter 1

Long Live the Queen

Bishop Fred Mattison died suddenly on a gray November evening, right after Thanksgiving. His membership at Center of Praise Church of God in Christ boasted over two hundred people. Most of them had been there since the seventies and eighties. They were an aging crowd that had held on to the traditional preaching and praying of Bishop Mattison. Although the membership hadn't grown, it had remained steady over the years. Deacons, Mothers, ushers, and musicians had praised God at Center of Praise since most of them could remember. Only the oldest members knew of a time when Bishop

Mattison wasn't pastor. However, it had been so long ago that everyone was afraid of what the future would hold.

There would be a vote. The elders in the church would be allowed to heavily campaign to become the next in leadership. They knew it would be a long, messy process. So many churches had broken up because of it. Center of Praise had heard of fights breaking out in the middle of church after someone who no one wanted was voted in.

Unfortunately, they had a huge problem that no one would be able to overlook. None of the men in the church had received their "Elder's License." This meant that no one was eligible to put their hat in the ring. Bishop Mattison had no children that were interested in the ministry, and he never appointed an assistant pastor. The only men with titles in the church were the deacons, who would only be able to vote someone else in and not become the next pastor themselves.

Several weeks following Bishop Mattison's funeral, several guest pastors came to show off their preaching talents, but none of them resonated with the membership. Some of them were too boisterous while others required too many offerings. Some were too young and inexperienced while others seemed like they were old enough to have actually been one of Jesus' disciples.

The church, still in the midst of grief because their perfect pastor would never show up again in the body of a talented, young minister of virtue, gave up their search. The deacon and mother's board decided to put their fate in the hands of the Bishop of the Southern California Jurisdiction. He would be able to appoint someone from the ranks of hundreds of young elders across Los Angeles and beyond. They knew this would mean that they might get someone from another state who didn't know anything about South Central Los Angeles, but most of the church decided it was worth it to take the risk.

Deacon Kingsley, a member of Center of Praise

since 1985, received a letter from Bishop Timothy Abernathy, head of the Southern California jurisdiction, on a stifling hot day in Los Angeles. Once he opened it, he thanked God that their prayers had been answered.

Dear Center of Praise,

I have located a lovely young minister to be appointed to your church. Sunday, June 15th, will be their first day. Please welcome them with open arms and with the love of Christ, our Lord and Savior. I will be making a visit to your location soon once they have settled and been installed. Bishop Mackenzie will be hosting the installation service that same day.

I look forward to meeting you all. Until then, may God bless and keep the Center of Praise Church of God in Christ.

Blessings from Our Savior,

Bishop Timothy J. Abernathy, Holiness Tabernacle Church of God in Christ

One of the other deacons caught him staring at the letter like he had won the lottery and asked what was wrong.

"We have found our pastor! Bishop Abernathy found one for us!"

"What if we don't like them?"

"I put my full faith and trust into Abernathy. He's always placed churches with that they were looking for. He wouldn't do us wrong."

"Let's only hope," the other deacon mumbled.

❖

Word passed around the church that they would be

getting their permanent pastor in two weeks. The common sentiment went from nervousness to excitement. Everyone tried to do their best to guess who it would be based on Bishop Abernathy's previous picks for other churches. Quite a few of the ladies had already bought brand new suits and hats to show to the potentially single minister. They knew Abernathy liked to place younger, unmarried men in these positions so they could better grow with the church.

The entire membership worked together to give the church a facelift before the arrival of their new pastor. Carpets were steamed, the stained glass windows were polished, and the garden outside was manicured to look like the cover of *Better Housekeeping.*

On the day of the pastor's arrival, members that hadn't been to the church in years waited to catch a glimpse of the installation ceremony that would take up one hour of service. The balcony above the auditorium was so full, they needed extra usher coverage for that day.

Bishop Mackenzie, who would be conducting the ceremony, arrived first with his entourage. Men in black suits and sunglasses followed him to the pulpit like the Secret Service.

Behind him walked in a woman who looked to be about forty years old, with shoulder length hair. She was brown-skinned and wore a well-fitting suit that inched toward her knees. A brimmed hat tilted to the side and partially shadowed her face. The purse she wore glided against her hips as she walked.

No one recognized her but she kept walking in the center of the aisle, keeping her eye contact off everyone. Bishop Mackenzie walked down from his seat and lifted his arm so she could hold on as Staci walked up the small set of stairs to the pulpit.

"Is that his wife? I thought he was married to someone else? Did she die?" were the whispers that could be heard buzzing in the crowd.

She could hear them, but gave the crowd a slight smile and stood next to the Bishop. She had a regal presence about her. Looking straight forward, she kept her gaze on Bishop Mackenzie as if waiting to be called into battle.

None of the members had ever seen a woman stand in the pulpit before. They had never witnessed a woman so confident around other men. It was like she was one of them, but in a skirt.

"Let the church say, Amen!" Bishop Mackenzie began. "Now, I know everyone is waiting for the big reveal. Isn't God good?"

"All the time! And all the time God is good!" the crowd echoed.

"Well, I won't delay the surprise any longer. However, I would like to introduce this person as one of the loveliest people I've ever met. They have their mind and heart on the love of the Lord. They have preached all over the world. This person has ministered in Jamaica, Nigeria, Ghana, and Puerto Rico. They're saved, sanctified, and filled with the Holy Ghost! They preach holiness or hell and aren't afraid to tell some of the saints that they need to stop sinning."

"Alright now!" a man in the crowd shouted.

"Center of Praise Church of God in Christ! I would like to introduce to you, your new shepherd, Pastor Staci Evangline Bernard! Let's put our hands together! Amen!"

Staci grabbed the mic and saw a sea of open mouths and nervous claps. Husbands looked at their wives and mothers grabbed their children. The mother's board was so still, the ushers wanted to check on them to make sure they weren't having a medical emergency.

Staci then heard a child whisper to his mother. The boy was in the second row, so she clearly saw him try to get his mother's attention while pointing.

"Mommy, it's a lady! Look!"

The mother, clearly embarrassed, mouthed that she was sorry and diverted her line of sight somewhere else.

Staci knew the crowd wasn't impressed, but this had been expected. She was trying to become a pastor in one of the most traditional church organizations that existed. She was also the first to do it. Bishop Abernathy had appointed her as the first female pastor of her church organization. Previously, women had only been allowed to be missionaries, evangelists, mothers in the church, and Sunday school teachers. However, this was the first time anyone in the church had ever seen a woman stand in the pulpit and not the podium on the main floor.

"Good morning, Center of Praise!"

An unenthused *"Good Morning"* from the people

followed.

"I am looking forward to being the pastor of this wonderful church. I have read and studied as much as I could about Bishop Mattison. God truly blessed that man to preach his word with such conviction. I know I have big shoes to fill but, with your help, I hope you will be willing to give me a chance to be the leader that you need me to be. I will preach the very same word this church had always treasured. I will make sure that the prayer line stays open. I want to maintain great relationships with all of you. I want to see the youth taking the church by storm. This is one of the greatest churches in Los Angeles. I grew up right here in Watts. I'm a local girl. I attended this church briefly as a teenager before I moved to Moreno Valley with my parents. However, there is no greater church than the grand ole' Church of God in Christ! Can I get an Amen!"

"Amen!"

Staci knew she had gained a little bit more of her

trust in just the few minutes she spoke to them. She saw shoulders start to relax, and the mother's board gave her slightly less of a side eye.

"You may be seated!"

She was a sweet faced, brown-skinned woman with straightened hair that sat on her shoulders. Her high cheekbones raised effortlessly when she smiled. Her hair had always been thick, but it was hard to manage when it was too long so she kept it at a shorter length. She wore minimal makeup, but always kept a coral lipstick on. It always highlighted her skin tone well. Staci had always been petite but at five feet six inches, she was slightly taller than the average woman. Traditional suits and hats lined her closet, so she knew she wouldn't have trouble fitting in. Although Staci enjoyed wearing sweat suits and jeans on a typical day, she knew that pants were not going to go over well with the traditionalists at Center of Praise.

Bishop Mackenzie led the installation service and

said a long-winded prayer that sent a few of those in the membership into an unintended slumber. The holy oil that always sat on the altar was placed on Staci's forehead in the shape of a cross. She then got on her knees and began to speak in tongues, asking God to guide her as she took the position of pastor.

The praise service followed, which increased the comfort level of the membership once again. However, most of those who had come just to see who the new pastor was left during offering. When she got up to preach, she was left with the most faithful two hundred who had been of service to Bishop Mattison for as long as they could remember.

Staci got up to preach following offering. She knew that they weren't looking for someone to be an exact copy of Bishop Mattison, but she knew some of the key topics church members would want to hear.

Pastor Bernard preached about love and all the

ways that people could show it unconditionally.

"Now saints, I know it may be hard to love those who may not love you. Jesus says that we should love our brothers and sisters. He meant everyone. He even means that one family member that cuts their eyes at you every time they see you. This doesn't mean that you have to spend time together every day. Love is respect. It is knowing that this person was still created by God and deserves to have compassion. You never know why people don't like you. A lot of times, it's because they have been hurt themselves. Pray for them. Just pray for people. God wants us to keep a prayer in our heart for others. Be genuine. God loves those that love him but, you better believe it, he still loves those who don't quite care for him, too."

Staci knew she had wooed most of the crowd. She had dozens of people standing and hanging onto her every word. A few of the deacons were still visibly upset. A few had gone into the back of the church until service was over.

The church began singing a congregational song following her sermon.

I get joy when I think about what he's done for me!
I get joy when I think about what he's done for me!
You can't tell it! Let me tell it!
What he's done for me!

Staci joined the worship by grabbing the nearest tambourine and then taking the lead to the song for a couple minutes.

Soon, the mother's board stood and all the deacons came out of hiding to witness what was going on. The entire church was on their feet. Staci came down from the pulpit and began to shout as the music changed to become faster paced.

A few joined her, and she held hands with them to pray once the music stopped.

It was one of the most memorable services Center of Praise had ever seen. The oldest members of the church still couldn't believe that it was a woman that had the church up and shouting for the first time since their revival last year. It was like she had lifted the church from a place of despair. Grief and anger began to dissipate from the minds of the membership. Some of them thought that they might truly learn to love Pastor Staci Bernard.

Offering came, and then the benediction.

God be with you!
Until we meet again!

The church sang their signature closing song, and then hundreds of parishioners lined up to shake Staci's hand and welcome her to the church.

Bishop Mackenzie bid her "goodbye" and walked out with his fleet of security. A few of the deacons tried to get his attention so they could ask a few more questions about where she came from. His security made them step back so he could enter his silver Maserati without problems.

What did she do for a living? Where was her husband? How many children did she have?

These were the questions spinning around in the heads of anyone in her presence. They thought she was pretty, sweet natured, and smart. However, other than that, she had no other footprints in Watts that they could research.

After only a handful of members were still at the church, Staci decided to give her social media information to the Sunday school teacher. The teacher, named Martha, was still in college trying to earn her degree to become an elementary school teacher.

"Thank you, Pastor Bernard. I'll send it to the older youth. I'm sure they'd like to connect with you!"

Staci shook her hand and promised to help her begin building an even larger youth program.

Just before Staci could lock the doors of the church two hours later and get in her car, she picked up her phone and saw that she had over one hundred notifications to befriend her on social media. She added them all, but she couldn't help but find it sweet that they were all trying to get to know her so quickly.

Hello All! Thank you for welcoming me to Center of Praise!

Staci said as a status message. Seventy-five likes followed within minutes.

"I think I'm going to like this church," Staci whispered to herself while driving the long way home. She hoped she could buy a house in Watts one day to be closer to the people.

Until then, social media would have to suffice.

❖

As the days went on, Staci became more comfortable with her position. It wasn't the easiest transition and, due to her being a woman, she felt that the deacons were making it intentionally harder. They told her that she would need to make sure several tasks were done before the following Sunday, such as making sure that the banking was done for the offering and that she opened the church on Wednesdays for prayer. Staci assured them several times that she knew what she was doing, but there was still some mild tension between herself and the deacons. She figured they would get over it.

Her social media page had more followers than she had ever anticipated. People were already sending her private messages asking for prayer and if she would do some favors for them such as officiate a wedding or Christening.

Staci was somewhat overwhelmed by the attention but she had worked for years to head her own church and, so far, most of the membership treated her with respect.

One of the oldest women at the church, Mother Earnestine Holloway, called her on Thursday night.

Staci barely heard her cellphone ring, but she answered it just in time.

The gravelly, weakened voice of an elderly woman began.

"Hello, Sister Bernard. This is Mother Earnestine."

Staci didn't feel like correcting a ninety-year old woman that she preferred to be called either Pastor Bernard or Pastor Staci. She just hoped the mistake wouldn't catch on. It was important to her that everyone in the church was given their correct title.

"Yes, hello Mother Holloway. How are you?"

"I'm doing just fine, baby. Well on Sunday, the women told me we gonna have a dinner after church to celebrate you. They wanted everybody to get together. Now they said it was gonna be a surprise, but I told them folks you can't sit up here and surprise no pastor. You need to tell folks or they might leave and gone 'bout they business."

Mother Earnestine's thick, southern accent comforted Staci. Her grandmother had passed away many years ago, so this was the first time she had a close relationship with an older person since then.

"Well, I'm so honored. I'll definitely be there. I'm looking forward to fellowshipping with all of you."

"Well, that's all I was gonna say. You sure did bring the message last Sunday."

"Thank you, ma'am."

"I'll be praying for you, baby," Mother Earnestine said weakly.

Staci ended the call and went to her closet to start organizing her church clothes. She was always conservatively dressed, but she wanted to include even more suits in her wardrobe to mirror what most of the women wore at City of Praise.

It was a possibility that she would wear a pastoral robe during communion and ceremonies. However, she didn't want to spring that on them quite yet. People were still getting used to having a woman as pastor and wouldn't be ready to embrace a woman looking exactly like the male pastor some of them still wished they had.

Her days were full of work now. Although the church was smaller than most, it needed a lot of oversight. Many of the departments had shrunk over the years, such as the youth department. In order for the church to grow, Staci would have to find a way to attract more young people. She had to find out how to do this while maintaining the integrity of the church.

By the time Sunday arrived, Staci was exhausted. She preached as she would every Sunday from now on but immediately after service, she went into the pastor's office to rest on her lounge chair.

Within ten minutes of her nap, she heard a knock at her door. It was one of the women from the mother's board.

Staci cracked the door open.

"Pastor, they're ready for you."

Staci put her heels back on and paced to the back of the church, where the dining room was. She removed her hat, but took her purse with her. Although she was now a pastor, Staci was determined to always look as feminine as possible.

She wore a red suit with a shimmering lapel. A gold cross pin was close to her collar. She began shaking hands as soon as she stepped into the dining room. Her seat was reserved for her at the head of the main table. Staci prayed over the dinner and then allowed the membership to get the food that was laid out buffet style.

She smiled so much, her cheeks began to hurt.

The mother's board kept a close eye on her like a hawk to its prey. The deacons finally came around to greet her once again but, this time, began to passive aggressively ask her questions in an attempt to quiz her about the Bible.

Staci had almost completed her Doctorate of Divinity, so she knew the Bible better than most people. She could quote scriptures like children knew their ABCs. Eventually, the deacons would stop questioning whether or not she knew "the word" well enough to teach it.

The Director of Hospitality, Anne Keys, placed a pile of food on a plate in front of her. Staci wondered why they hadn't asked her about her potential food restrictions and allergies, but then she realized that this was Watts and large meals like this were scarce for many of her members.

Staci thanked her and began eating while talking to most of the older women. It wasn't the most comfortable feeling, but then a seat opened between two women for the Sunday school teacher to sit down. She and Staci began to talk since they knew they would have more in common. Martha was twenty-seven years old, but very mature for her age.

"Pastor Bernard, you said that you wanted to improve the youth department. What is one of the things you are going to tackle first?" Martha began.

Suddenly, a hush fell on the table. Everyone's ears

were locked in on what Staci would say.

"Well, I spoke to a couple of the young people this morning and it looks like they would enjoy having a praise dance team."

Staci watched the elderly mother's board gasp in unison. The old pastor banned praise dancing because he felt that they were unnecessary and had people "dancing out of the spirit."

"Oh, I don't know if the young people would need that. We've never danced in church except under the guidance of the Holy spirit."

"Yes, I understand, Mother Holloway. However, we have so much talent just sitting here at church and a praise dance team encourages teamwork, exercise, music education, and holiness all in one."

"Now, how is dancing out the spirit holy?" Mother

Jackson murmured under her breath with a mouth full of food.

"I know many of you aren't keen on change, but I promise that this will be a wonderful way to introduce the church to the amazing talents of the youth. Most churches have a praise or flag team now. All they do is add beauty to worship. They won't take away from the spiritual dancing. Besides, I've seen some praise dancers get engrossed in the spirit and then start shouting after a performance. You never know how this art form might touch somebody."

Martha smiled at her answer and decided to talk about a few more church-related topics until the two began talking about their experiences in college. The Mothers' Board eventually tuned them out.

Staci felt a tap on her shoulder a few minutes later. She looked in both directions until she saw a man who appeared closer to her age smile with his hand outstretched. Staci shook his hand. His handshake was firm and genuine. He had kind eyes and slightly receding hairline.

He introduced himself as Todd Jenkins. He had been the church organist and pianist for the past fifteen years. As soon as she stood to greet him, her five-inch heels allowed her to almost tower over his thin, five-feet-seven inch frame.

"I just wanted to personally welcome you, Pastor Bernard. I hadn't gotten the chance to say anything. I've really enjoyed the preaching these last two Sundays. If you ask me, Bishop Mattison would be proud."

"Thank you so much, I truly appreciate it."

"I'm one of the musicians. I've been here for about fifteen years."

He wore gold rimmed glasses and his striped

collared shirt was wrinkled. He reminded her of a slightly older Urkel from the TV show *Family Matters*. He had a patchy beard and had an overwhelming cologne scent that Staci was still able to smell long after he left her side.

"Well, you sure do know how to play. Thank you for backing me up these last two Sundays. Now, I'm not one of those preachers that needs an A-flat at the end of my message to end it, but I have my own style."

"No, Pastor," he laughed. "You're doing a great job. I can't wait to see what else is in store. I'll be praying for you."

Staci shook his hand once again and then sat down. She saw Martha try to hide rolling her eyes. A couple of the women she sat next to shook their heads.

"Well, he's very nice. He's very talented, too," Staci uttered.

"He is. He can just be a little irritating sometimes. He's been trying to get the youth department off the ground for a while," Martha said with her eyes still gazing down at her food.

"Why is that annoying? He sounds ambitious."

Staci ended that conversation topic and picked up where they left off talking about college. She guessed that Todd was like that annoying nerd in high school that always asked you out to the school dances, but you'd rather go with anyone else but him.

Following the dinner, Staci gave a "thank you" speech and led a prayer for everyone before they left.

She shook the hands of dozens more before she finally retired in her office for the next hour. Resting her eyes in an empty church was peaceful and relaxing to her. She always felt the glory of God around her whenever she was in his house of worship. Staci had always loved being in church for as long as she could remember. When other teenagers were trying to find any excuse to get out of going to church, Staci always found a way to participate more.

From being an usher to a youth missionary, Staci still loved putting in more work for the Lord. Now, she was able to do it full-time. She had a job as a secretary for a shipping company to support her while she earned her degree, but wouldn't need it anymore. Never, in her wildest dreams, did she expect to be fully supported by her dream job as a pastor.

Following other pastors on social media and networking with them became another aspect of her job. She wanted to know more about what some of the most popular pastors in the nation did to grow their church. Her dream was to increase the membership roll by more than three-hundred in two years. Unfortunately, Watts had also begun to see an exodus of African Americans to the desert areas for cheaper housing. More Hispanics had moved in to replace them. To keep up, Staci was going to figure out how to create more inclusive services that were in English and Spanish. The youth department needed more outlets to attract more young people to a rapidly aging church. The church could use a guitarist and sound technician instead of relying on Todd for everything.

It was going to be a lot of work, but Staci knew she was up for the challenge.

Her mother and father congratulated her on leading her own church. Her father, a former traveling minister, felt proud that his daughter had gotten to do what he had once imagined for himself.

"You know they're going to try to mess with you because you're a woman. You got to ignore those devils."

"I know, Dad," Staci answered while talking to him on the phone that Sunday evening.

"They think that just because you're a woman, you'll

make decisions based on emotion."

"And I know it's not true but they can think what they want. I'll just have to pray for them."

"Although, I do wish my baby girl had some help."

"As in what? I have a whole deacon's board that won't let me carry out any decision without putting it past them first."

"No. I mean a family. You were always moving around so much that you must have forgotten that God wants us to be blessed with family, too."

Her father's sickly yet deep voice trailed through the receiver of the phone like she was hearing bad news from the doctor's office. She tried to keep a single tear from falling out of her eye. She always wanted a partnership, but she knew that having a family would get in the way of her missionary work and education. She had been able to quickly rise in the ranks of an organization that shunned women as leaders. She was like the Hilary Clinton of the black church.

However, the first rule of the game was not admitting weakness. No one at church missed a "Mr. Bernard," so she assumed it wasn't necessary. Besides, Staci thought that at forty-years-old, she wasn't exactly the young flower men were running after. Although many people thought she was at least five to seven years younger than she really was, she could feel that men were intimidated by a woman that was a world traveling missionary, a minister, a youth pastor, an assistant pastor, and later the pastor of her own church. Staci was sure that men wanted a more docile woman that would make a beautiful first lady to sit in the front row. She was never the type of woman to sit and look pretty, so finding a saved man that understood her aspirations might be difficult.

Her heart still longed for companionship but, at the moment, she was married to Jesus and hopefully, the rest of the church would see and understand where her heart was.

Chapter 2

Rumor Has It

Fear swept through the church that Center of Praise would shrink in size. A woman pastor was bound to subtract from their solid two-hundred-person membership. Bishop Mattison could barely hold on to the faithful members he inherited, so surely Staci Bernard would run the people away.

Those members were wrong, and Pastor Bernard even managed to get new families to the church in a short period of time. Everyone was interested in the woman who would preach you "happy." No one had seen anything like it. Although she had a softer voice and her lipstick was always smeared somewhere on the microphone, more of her membership began to embrace her. The young people loved how she actually listened to them. They finally felt part of the church and not just there to be seen and not heard.

Over time, even though she was doing her best to make friends, she noticed many of the women in the church held on to their husbands a little bit tighter when she walked past them. Men found her attractive but they were either too old, too feminine, or already married. The women who were married saw her as competition, but the single women pitied her.

They saw her as someone that was also in their position of loneliness. Staci looked content, but many wondered how any woman could truly be happy without a partner.

It seemed like each Sunday, the whispers concerning her relationship status were getting louder and more frequent. It didn't matter that many of the soundbites from her sermons had gone viral on several Christian platforms, or that she was an accomplished author on her way to receiving her doctorate, and even one of the most accomplished women the church had ever seen. She was single and that would always make her a target for disdain.

Martha, who had become one of her good friends, told Staci that she had heard rumors about her being a lesbian. She warned her that people had even gone as far as to link her to women that had also moved up in rank in the Church of God in Christ.

One night, Staci had been so bothered by the lesbian rumors that she started crying in her office. She had been reflecting on biblical passages in one of her devotionals and then broke down in tears. All the stress from leading such a large church and the lack of a partner to help her take on the load was beginning to take a toll on her.

Staci knew that most of the people were just curious, but there were several others that just wanted to find something negative to say. They were the same people that wished they had been given a male pastor and felt that Staci was some kind of cruel mistake.

She had always wanted a husband and family for years but it had never worked out. Friends, parents, and classmates had tried to hook her up for a while. The men they introduced her to were never her type. Staci knew that there had to be a man out there that was well dressed, tall, handsome, financially stable, and saved. Every night, she prayed that God would send her the man she both wanted and needed. The men she ran into in public would fit one category, but not the others. The men that she really clicked with were pastors themselves and wanted a docile first lady by their side. Few men wanted to be "First Man" or "First Husband" of anyone's church. It was considered emasculating, and she knew they would fight for some other title so it wouldn't look like she was above them. Many men were intimidated by her educational background. She had graduated from high school early, going on to study at Berkeley and then graduate school at the University of Southern California. Her Doctorate of Divinity degree was well within reach.

The churches she had visited over the years allowed her to meet men of all races and backgrounds. Non-Black men never caught her interest and she wasn't interested in someone who wasn't at least Baptist. She found out she had little in common with Methodists and Episcopalians. Besides, her parents would feel like she had left "the faith" if she went on to marry a non-Pentecostal man.

Every time she wanted to talk to someone about what was going on, she had to call up a friend or her parents. Just once, she wanted to be able to share her most intimate thoughts with a man that would hug her and remind her that everything would be okay. Everyone always knew her as the strongest Black woman around, but Staci didn't always feel that way. A lot of time, she felt weak. Just once, she just wanted to admit to a man she loved that she enjoyed being a pastor, but it got hard sometimes. That was something she afraid to admit to anyone else for fear that she would appear ungrateful.

Once Staci's tears dried up and she felt a bit better, she wrote down in a journal what she desired in a man once again. She got on her knees with the journal on her bed and prayed to God that he would send her the man she needed to help her carry the burden of a church.

"Lord, I need a husband. I am asking you to send me an upstanding man that honors you in every way. Send me someone who can help me in your ministry. Send someone who wants to encourage me and allow me to have a full family. I know you can do it, Lord. You have done so much for me and I know you can send someone that wants to do right by you and give me a pure love. I will wait for your answer and I know that when I see it, I will be so blessed. Amen."

Staci put her journal away and changed into her night clothes. Although she was the only one in the house, she still enjoyed wearing silk pajamas and robes in beautiful colors.

To get her mind off her desire for a husband, she decided to dive into her plans for the youth department. While in bed, she wrote down a few plans she would introduce to Martha, who has just been promoted to President of the Youth Department.

Praise dancing as well as service just for the young people was outlined in her plans. She wanted the youth to do more outreach, and she wanted to invite a youth minister to come and speak at least once a month. She thought it was time to hire more musicians that could play more updated songs. Their church didn't even have a youth choir that practiced often. She wanted to have both a children's and teen choir.

Her eyelids began to fall and she put her notebook away to finally fall asleep. She turned off the light on her nightstand and slept on the left side of her bed only. She didn't even stretch her legs out the other side of the bed. Even though there was no one there, it made her feel good to pretend that she had to share her King-sized bed sometimes.

❖

"Now, this sounds nice!" Todd said enthusiastically during the Youth and Music Department meeting Staci held on Saturday. "We need to go out and search for some more young musicians. I know Randy isn't gonna like that, but we could use an update. I hear those new churches have drum machines now to fill in the sound."

Mother Holloway rolled her eyes and interjected. "Well, we have never needed that much music. You're going to blow the roof off this place. I also still don't agree with the praise dancing. Bishop Mattison would have never approved."

"Well, Bishop Mattison is gone, Mother Holloway," Todd said under his breath.

Mother Holloway wasn't supposed to be at the meeting but once she heard that a church discussion meeting was being held without her, she insisted that she be part of it.

Staci had to be more careful about what she shared with everyone because of her presence.

"I know he's gone! That don't mean we got to let the devil in the church!"

"Mother Holloway," Martha interrupted. "We're just going to try it out. If the church doesn't respond well to it, then we'll try something else."

"Also," Staci continued. "I would like to propose that we have our first all-youth service next month. I was going to invite a youth minister, young soloists, have the young people lead prayer, announcements and everything. This will be a wonderful opportunity to get some fresh, young talent in the church."

"Fresh young talent? We got enough talent. A lot of young people don't take God seriously," Mother Holloway sneered.

Brother Joe, the bassist who had been a member at the church since the seventies, chimed in. He was always surly and never spoke to anyone much unless it was an insult. Rumor had it that he had made Todd cry once. Bishop Mattison wanted to fire him several times, but he refused to leave.

"I don't know why we're taking all these directions from somebody who don't even know our church," Brother Joe groaned.

"Brother Joe, this is our pastor. You should show more respect," Todd said.

"I am showing respect. Does her husband know this is how she talk to people?"

"I-I'm not married," Staci said, trying to keep her composure.

"Well, I can see why. You trying to run everybody around here. Men don't like that." Brother Joe hissed.

"Now, you need to be quiet. This is God's house. Keep it holy," Martha interjected.

"Well at least *you* act like a woman. You'll find somebody. This one here think she a man."

Staci felt the tears freeze in her eyes. She was doing everything in her power to keep herself from running out of the room. As a pastor, she was supposed to take the heat from the membership. If she didn't, people would consider her weak and try to get her out the position. Bishop Abernathy had trusted her to be able to lead the people without getting emotional.

"I'm going to have to ask you to leave, Brother Joe," Staci commanded.

"Where? This *my* church."

"It's our church, and we want you to leave," Todd added.

"Leave? Fine! I might not come back. Find another bassist who will work for the low pay y'all give out! I don't wanna deal with no lesbian running the church no how!"

Everyone in attendance gasped and watched Brother Joe storm out of the auditorium. Todd followed to make sure he was out the door.

Martha ran up to the podium to rub Staci's shoulder. "Pastor, I'm so sorry. He's never been this hostile before, but he's always had issues. We never knew what to do with him. He insults everyone."

"It's okay." Staci felt a single tear come down her cheek and then addressed the audience. "You know what, I was going to try to hide this but I won't. My feelings are hurt. I'm a human being. I'm a child of God and all I do is try to get people saved and closer to our God. I haven't done anything to deserve this, but I'll use this as a teachable moment. Sometimes, a bad spirit will come in the church to test you. That spirit will catch you when you least expect it. It's happened to so many men and women in the Bible. Yes, I am a woman. But, I am your pastor and I demand as much respect as you gave Bishop Mattison. I hope I made myself clear?"

"Yes, Pastor," the attendees said in unison.

The meeting continued with the business of the church, such as how they would raise money. Mother Holloway stayed quiet for the remainder of the meeting. She quietly took notes without giving Staci too much eye contact.

"I would like to introduce to you, the young lady that I have chosen to teach praise dancing at Center of Praise. Her name is Amisha and she is a trained dancer. I'm sure many of you all didn't know that. I want to bring her talents to this here stage. This is the greatest stage in the world."

Amisha meekly walked up to the podium and gave a short speech about her plans for the praise dance team.

"Would you give us an example of one of the dances you plan on showing our girls?" Staci asked from the first pew.

"Yes, Pastor."

Amisha asked Todd to set up the music on the speakers from her phone. "Let the Church Say Amen" by Andraé Crouch played over the church's sound system.

Mother Holloway shook her head and walked out of the church.

Martha giggled and immediately stood up to support her cousin.

Amisha dazzled the audience with her twists, turns, and intricate steps. She used a ribbon as a prop and was able to interact with the audience at different times during the song. She used some sign language to follow the lyrics.

Staci cried and stood up at the end of her performance. Amisha was overwhelmed by hugs and handshakes from her audience of twenty-five.

Staci took the microphone once again.

"Look, church. This here is what happens when you allow the young people to take over. Change is good sometimes. It can be scary, but don't you see what happens when we allow the youth to do what God has called them to do? The youth aren't here to just sit in the front row and copy the mother's and deacon's board. They're here to be a joy. Jesus loved the little children. We should as well. I would like to get a show of hands of all those who would like to add praise dancing to our youth line-up."

An enthusiastic crowd raised their hands with one-hundred percent agreement.

Staci recorded their vote and concluded the meeting with a prayer. Directly following the meeting, the feeling in the air was still tense. Martha tapped Staci on the shoulder while everyone else was leaving.

"I'm so sorry about what happened. You really turned it around, though. That man is the devil."

"No, he just has some spirit in him. I won't take what he said to heart."

Martha gave her another hug and left the auditorium a few minutes later.

The large church was silent. Only the sounds of trees rustling outside could be heard. Her heart sank deeper into her chest and a stray tear traveled down her cheek once again.

"Jesus, help me," she whispered. "Just help me."

The click clack of her heels echoed down the aisle and she locked the doors until they would reopen Sunday morning. The church was wonderful, but she was still waiting on an answer from her heart's most desperate prayer.

Pastor Bernard was becoming known as one of the best preachers in the city. She could compete with the men and have crowds standing up within minutes. Her time in theology school had allowed her to master the topics that most African American crowds wanted to hear.

Services became livelier. Center of Praise was shouting every Sunday. Pastor Bernard danced through the aisles and spoke in tongues. She prayed for the sick and asked God for breakthroughs. Several months later, the membership began to fully embrace Staci and many of the newest members had only been under the guidance of a female pastor.

Staci had encouraged Martha to set up the first annual Youth Day. She had invited a youth minister from Long Beach and praise dancers from another church. The youth were scheduled to lead the offering, prayer, announcements, and benediction.

The mother's board had calmed down, but they still had a look of skepticism on their faces. They still weren't comfortable with the young people potentially disrupting the service.

The praise dancers were well received and the youth minister had even the youngest children shouting down the aisle. They raised more money during the Youth Day offering than they raised during regular services. The deacons had told Staci that they were sure the offering would be less than half of what they were used to receiving.

The benediction came, and then Martha announced to everyone that there would be cake and punch after service to celebrate.

Staci stayed after service a bit to shake the hands of several of the youth performers. Brother Joe rolled his eyes when she glanced at him. She had the power to fire him right then and there, but she didn't think it was worth it. Staci knew that God would be the last to judge him and his actions. It would be best to greet him with pure kindness for now and pray for his soul later.

After church, Staci and Martha sat together. Staci saw her scroll through her phone and then when she put it down, a picture of her and a young man lit up on her screensaver.

"Who's that young man?"

"My boyfriend. Well, hopefully we'll be fiancés soon."

Staci took a sip of her punch. "You're hoping that he'll propose soon?"

"Well, I don't know when but I know it's going to happen. He's such an amazing man. He comes from a good family and we're both ready to settle down. I really don't want to wait until I'm forty to have kids."

Staci saw Martha nervously look over and she touched her shoulder. "I mean, I'm sorry. I've heard of so many women who have kids later. It's just that all this pressure from my mom and stuff..."

"No. I understand. I totally understand. I just got too busy in my career and now with a job like this, I don't know who would have time for me."

"I'm sure plenty of men would. Not all men are looking for women that they can control or have by their side to have as simple arm candy. My boyfriend loves that I have my own career and have ambitions of becoming a principal."

"Well, once you hit my age, it's not that easy," Staci said, eating a bite of chocolate cake. "The men are either old, married, or crazy."

"I wouldn't be too sure about that, Pastor. Besides, there are so many people around your age that go online now. I have an aunt that met her husband on a Christian dating site. I feel like God allows technology to be used for his glory as well. He's the sweetest man. A lot of people might look at them sideways because they met online, but it's really no one's business."

"Online? I don't think too many people are on there

like that."

"Yes, you just haven't been on there yet. I was skeptical at first, but my aunt found an actual Christian man."

"I'll think about it. I don't know yet. I asked God to send me a husband. The Bible says that a *'man who findeth a wife'* and not the other way around."

"Well, don't knock it until you try it, Pastor Bernard," Martha said with a smile, picking up her plate to take it back to the kitchen.

❖

The following week, Staci found a few extra minutes to scroll through her social media account. She liked to catch up on what her membership was doing and send them words of encouragement.

Five minutes into liking pictures, she came across Martha's surprise proposal that was held at a restaurant. Martha was tagged in a photo of her boyfriend, Timothy, placing a diamond ring on her finger.

Staci thought it was one of the most beautiful moments she had ever seen. Martha was shocked and began crying as she hugged Timothy around his neck once she accepted the ring.

Martha took several other pictures with the ring and posed with her family.

Tears began to stream down Staci's face. She had to grab a few tissues while looking at the loving couple. Grabbing her bathrobe, she lit a scented candle and stretched out on her bed. She closed her eyes and allowed the scent of the candle cover the room.

Staci couldn't tell if she was crying because she was happy for Martha or secretly envious. Martha had tried her best to talk to her about online dating and uplift her with the hope of finding the one. She wondered if it was a possibility that she had pushing away too many men that meant well. Online dating seemed scary, but it was possibly the way that God wanted to put her husband in front of her.

Staci pulled her laptop onto her bed and went to the African American Christian singles website that Martha had mentioned to her once. Her heart was racing as she clicked on the website. Staci looked around as if someone could walk in at any moment and catch her searching on a website that she knew most pastors never used. Most pastors were married, and the ones who were single always had rumors swarming behind their back. Staci, even though she was a woman, was no exception. The rumors still swirled, but she just knew how to ignore them better.

Her age, weight, occupation, and a short blurb about herself started her profile out. She did not want to put a picture up yet until she could take a new one. There were a lot of selfies on her phone, but none of them showed off her figure or angles in the best way.

She paid for a monthly membership, which gave her instant access to the men on the website that were available. Her profile wasn't active yet, but she was allowed to peruse through a few profiles. Many of the men were too old for her and plenty were divorced with adult kids. She didn't mind being with someone that was divorced, but she had heard of a lot of men having messy divorces that ended up with even worse heartbreak.

Her rules remained at not wanting a man with young children. She also wasn't interested in another pastor that had their own church. She knew that would interfere with her church. They might want her to leave her position and become their First Lady.

The profiles seemed promising. She filtered her search to someone between thirty-five and fifty-five years old. Southern California was her primary area to search, but she was open to dating someone that lived in Northern California or a state close by, such as Nevada.

Staci wondered if she was going against God by searching for her husband, but she remembered the story of Ruth and how she put herself in front of Boaz to be seen. Ruth later became his wife and was one of the most revered women in the Bible. Staci had never been taught to sit back and let things happen. Besides, her parents always taught her that faith without works is dead.

The evening grew darker as Staci developed a potential list of suitors that she would contact once her profile was complete. She felt like a teenager getting to know her first crush. The open world of online dating kept her attention all night long. She wondered why Martha hadn't suggested this before. Some of the men were exceptionally handsome and had well-written profiles that let her know they were at least literate.

Her mother called her around eight o'clock in the

evening. She usually called on Sunday evenings, so Staci closed her laptop and answered her call.

"Hello?" Staci answered.

"How have you been doing, Staci?" Her mother's southern drawl made her feel like a little girl all over again. Her voice was the sound of gravy on warm mashed potatoes during a Sunday dinner.

Her parents were in their seventies and lived in Las Vegas after home prices in California began to increase far beyond their income.

"I've been doing well. The church has been growing and shouting. Folks are getting saved and God is just blessing!"

"Well, that's good to hear. Jesus can work, if you let him. Now, you sounded a little pre-occupied when I first called. Were you doing something?"

"No. Not really."

Staci laid her laptop on her nightstand and closed her window to stop the cool breeze from coming through.

"Not talking to anyone?"

"Talking to who? The members? A friend? No, not anyone. Not right now."

She heard her mother sigh. Her father was loudly snoring in the background. He still worked at the post office because he wouldn't retire. More than likely, he was just getting some extra sleep in before his long shift in the morning.

"Is that Daddy?" Staci asked.

"Yes, that's your father. He in here snoring like an engine. Good gracious a life!"

"Now, have any young men at the church tried to say anything to you?"

"Mother, we've been over this. I'm not talking to anyone right now. I'm trying to get my church in order. I'm doing God's work first, and then I'll worry about my personal life."

"You've been so worried about your career for years. Every man we put in front of you, you don't care for."

Her mother paused. "You not no lesbian, are you?"

"Mother! Have I ever shown interest in women?"

"No, you haven't, but it's just that people start wondering when you refuse to marry."

"I never refused to marry. God has not sent me my husband. I have remained pure and have never let a man into my house that I wasn't married to. I have held myself

69

accountable to the Lord all these years, and all y'all want to do is criticize me. There aren't thousands of men banging down my door. It was never like that."

"You are a beautiful woman, Staci. Don't talk about yourself like that. I never had no ugly child."

"I never said that. It's just that once you get a certain age and in a certain position in life, the men are not as plentiful. I know you're going to talk about all those men you wanted me to meet over the years, but I'm not trying to raise a man. I want a man who has his life together and values me."

"Frederick didn't value you?"

"No, mother. He thought he was prettier than me. He was always talking about my weight and had more to say about my nail color than spending time with me. You know something was wrong with that man."

Her mother stayed silent on the phone for a few seconds and then cleared her throat. "A woman needs help in this life, Staci."

"You don't think I see that? I know!" Staci shrieked. She never yelled at her mother before, but the tears wouldn't stop coming. She'd rather yell than cry.

"I'll let you do what you were doing. I don't have the time to be arguing with no negro on the phone. I'll be praying for you."

Her mother hung up abruptly.

Staci slammed her head into her pillow and let the tears flow as much as she wanted for the next half-hour.

Staci loved what she did. Not having a husband was not going to take away from the success she had amassed thus far. A radio interview and being one of the featured speakers at next year's Holy Convocation was on the horizon. Part of her wondered if having a family sooner would have impeded her progress. Most of the time, women had to make more sacrifices for men for the same position and less money.

Her God had blessed her with the ability to be a full-time pastor without having to take on a job. He had allowed her to rise above all the demonic spirits in the church that were waiting for her to fail. She knew that there was no way God would fail her now.

She picked up her laptop and opened it so the dating website she was on reappeared. Staci took a deep breath and began writing more about herself. Her politics, favorite food, favorite animal, and places she wanted to travel to were all on display. Within an hour, she had filled out more than three quarters of her profile.

Staci scrolled down the photo album in her phone, trying to find an appropriate picture to put on her profile. Her mind began to wander into all kinds of "what ifs." She wondered if someone from church would see this and judge her. There were other single people at church but hopefully, not enough of them that they happened to be one of the thousands of profiles on the website.

While scrolling through her album a few more seconds, Staci came across a picture of herself in a red and white suit she wore for Valentine's Day. It was clear and revealed her smile. There was no one else in the picture, and it looked like she was standing in a church. Staci thought that would be the perfect picture to place on her profile. She wanted more, but the red and white suit picture would have to suffice.

Her profile was mostly finished, so she made it public.

She said a short prayer and asked God to work through this platform.

"In Jesus' name, Amen."

Chapter 3

Love At Last

The Youth Department decided to have a celebratory dinner at a local buffet restaurant. Martha, Todd, and the new praise dance team were in attendance. Staci made an appearance, but came late because she had to attend a finance meeting with the deacons right after church.

Staci sat next to Martha, who usually knew how to have the most conversation. Staci was naturally shy during one-on-one interactions, so Martha was better at being able to get everyone to talk and joke.

Todd sat on her right, which slightly irritated her. He was always trying to make conversation but ended up coming off as corny and sometimes inconsiderate. He was an intelligent man and meant well. He was also kind to everyone and always had brilliant ideas. However, there was nothing about him that screamed "husband" or even "boyfriend" to her. He lacked the masculine, commanding vibe that she craved in a partner. Todd was saved and sanctified, but he felt like he could be a friend or even her brother.

Once most of the dinner guests left, including Todd, Martha and Staci began talking about more non-church related topics.

"So, Todd isn't that much younger than you. I think he's thirty-eight."

"What's that supposed to mean?" Staci said, taking another sip of her iced tea.

"He's on fire for the Lord. I know that's right."

"A lot of men are on fire for Jesus. That doesn't mean

that I need to marry them. Besides, I took your advice about the online dating thing."

Martha's eyes widened. "Really? What happened? Who did you meet?"

"Oh, I just got on there. I barely put my picture up. I haven't gone back to see who's interested."

"Did you go on the Black Christian Singles one?"

"Yes. It's not so bad so far. I saw a few men I'd be interested in on there. I thought there were going to be a whole lot of rejects."

"See, that's why I told you to give it a chance, Pastor."

"Well, I won't get my hopes up too much. It's just a little diversion for when I'm not as busy. I won't think about it too much."

❖

Following her long drive home, Staci logged onto her account within five minutes of walking into the door. She had been secretly hoping that she had received a message all day. She had read recent article that talked about how difficult it was for Black women to find someone online. Men tended to stereotype Black women and overlook them for women of another race or ethnic background.

Her heart was racing as she logged onto the website. She felt like she walking into a strange universe every time her username and password were accepted.

Instantly, there were already a dozen messages waiting for her. She clicked on the first one. It was a fifty-five-year old man that served as an usher at his church. He had recently divorced with no children and was looking to connect with someone special.

Staci was not immediately attracted him due to his receding hairline and droopy eyes. He also started his message with a Bible scripture. It would have been romantic if he hadn't started out with the verse that commanded that wives obey their husbands. She assumed he was also new to online dating and had no idea what he was doing.

A few of the other men seemed promising, but one of them had three young children and another said he had recently been delivered of homosexuality.

Some of the messages were hilarious, but others were sad because she could feel the desperation in their short bio. Staci wondered what the ladies side of the website looked like if this was all the men had to offer.

Sadness overcame her when she realized she had no messages left. All the men that had messaged her were not her type.

Staci filled out more of her profile and added more detail to her bio. She even added two more selfies that she had taken the day before. They were brighter and were more of a close-up. She wasn't a heavy social media person, but she noticed that a lot of the women liked to take pictures of just their faces with lots of make-up. Staci had done her make-up extra nicely that day, just to take a few photos that she would like to put on display on her profile.

While browsing the website, she decided to go into the search function and look for someone she might be interested in talking to. It was a dating website for both men and women, so she figured that it was fine if she decided to start searching for men instead of letting them search for her.

Staci put everything she desired in the filters. Their height had to be over six feet. They had to be Pentecostal or at least Baptist, never married, no children, didn't smoke, didn't drink, and were politically conservative.

Her search yielded just three results and of those three, her heart almost stopped when she clicked on his profile.

His name was Marcus and he was exactly forty years old and reminded her of the actor Morris Chestnut. He had a bald head, a full beard, and eyes that focused on the camera as if he had modeled before. He was six-feet-three inches tall and muscular. He had pictures wearing a suit and others with a T-shirt on, laying down on the couch. He claimed he didn't drink or smoke and led a healthy lifestyle. There were several pictures of him in the gym lifting weights, and he said that he tried to drink at least half a gallon of water every day.

Marcus was a traveling minister and was working on getting his elder's license with the Church of God in Christ. He was born into church and had never stopped attending. He said he had always been on the lookout for a faithful wife and hadn't found the "Ruth to his Boaz" yet. Although he had never married, he admitted that he was "very interested" in tying the knot soon. He wanted children, but was okay if that didn't happen.

He checked absolutely every box on Staci's list.

However, he was traveling all the time and she wanted someone who wouldn't mind sticking around one city for a long period of time. She didn't want to have a husband that was always gone like he was in the military.

Staci wanted to message him, but she was afraid to make the first move. She had always been told that a woman should wait on the man to chase her. If she did it backward, she hoped that God would still be open to blessing her potential union with this man.

Taking a deep breath, she clicked on the icon that allowed someone to send him a message. She closed her eyes and visualized what she was going to say. This was the type of man you didn't meet every day, so she didn't want to mess it up.

Hello,

I was reading your profile and you definitely seem like a man on fire for Jesus. I see you like to play tennis from time to time. I used to play in high school, but maybe you could help me brush up on some skills. I see you're a minister as well. I'm also in the ministry and have been a member of the grand ol' Church of God in Christ since I was a baby. There isn't any other church like it.

You seem like someone fun to be around, so I thought I would send a message first. If my profile strikes your fancy as well, please message me back. I'd be delighted to talk to you.

Staci

She read her message about ten times before she sent it. Her nerves were sending moisture into her fingers and allowing tiny beads of sweat to build up on her keys. There was a possibility that Marcus would see her message and ignore it because he never answered messages from women. Thoughts of not being pretty enough for him swam through her head, and she wondered if there were too many pictures of her dressed up for church and not in casual clothes.

Staci wanted to tell someone what she did so badly, but she was afraid of word getting out that she was dating online like "those sinful young folk." Instead, she waited for his response by closing her laptop and starting her dinner for the evening. Then, she remembered that the website had an app you could download on your phone. Staci found the app and then downloaded it. She logged in and allowed notifications to be sent directly to her. The sounds for phone notifications was turned on.

Two hours later, Staci began to get more anxious. She had already cooked and caught up with church business that she handled over text. There was nothing else left for her to do. She turned the TV on to take her mind off everything, but then her eyes began to get heavy. It was almost time for bed, but part of her still had hope that Marcus would notify her.

She went on the app and hoped that maybe his message

had just gotten lost or her phone hadn't picked it up.

There was nothing.

Once her night clothes were on and she turned on the heater in her room, she hoped that she would finally be able to relax in bed.

The anxiety wouldn't allow her to go straight to sleep. Marcus' pictures and her message kept spinning around in her head.

She was sure he had read the message and decided that she wasn't worth talking to. He probably looked at her pictures and preferred someone younger, prettier, and less "churchy" looking. Thoughts of defeat came to her and then she tried to shut out the thoughts by turning on some Gospel music and letting her mind drift away.

The music that was coming from her phone was suddenly interrupted by the loud bell sound she had on her phone that played when she got a message or a notification.

Staci sprang up from her bed like it was an emergency to grab her phone.

It read: **You have a message!**

Staci opened the app and saw that Marcus had, indeed, replied to her. His paragraph was almost as long as hers.

Staci,

Thank you for messaging me! I don't go on here as often as I used to, but I'm so glad I logged on tonight. Yes, I am an avid tennis player. I also play basketball and coach the youth at my local gym. Yes, I am a minister. I don't have a church yet, but I'm working on getting my license so I can become a pastor. You are such a beautiful woman. I love your smile. You look like you're modeling those clothes. What is it that you do in the church?

Marcus

Staci felt like a giddy school girl all over again. It was like the first taste of candy after leaving the candy store as a child. She felt like she had won something.

Marcus sounded intelligent. He was able to write a full paragraph without making any grammatical mistakes. She wondered where he had gone to college, but that part of his profile was empty.

When she decided to reply, Staci thought about how she would answer his last question. Should she tell him that she was a pastor? Although he was in the church, he might be intimidated by her. She was proud of her position, but being ahead of men had been a problem in her dating life before.

Staci decided that she would tell him that she was simply in leadership at her church and worked in the ministry. Of course, churches had several different types of ministries you could be in, but Staci figured he wouldn't ask any more questions about it. When she got to know him better, she planned on telling him about her position as pastor of one of the largest COGIC memberships in South Los Angeles.

She messaged him back immediately, but tried to keep it shorter this time.

Marcus,

You sure know how to compliment, don't you? I sure do wish I was a model, but I've gotten too old for it now. I'm part of the leadership in my church, but I'm heavy in the ministry. I believe that God wants us to serve him in any way we can. Whether it's with the youth department or hospitality, I always like to be of service. What church do you attend mainly?

Staci

Marcus replied fifteen minutes later.

Staci,

I go to New City Church of God in Christ but, like

I said, I'm all over the place; Bishop Randall is my pastor. I'm starting to wrap up here at the church. We had a function that lasted a little longer than expected. I might not be able to talk for the rest of the night. However, let me give you my number. Call me around nine in the morning. I'd love to continue this conversation off the app.

Marcus

323-555-2173

Staci programmed his number into her phone and then felt a rush of relief. Marcus was actually interested in her and wanted to even call instead of text. She knew a lot of men today wanted to text instead of call. Hopefully, he would sound as articulate on the phone as he sounded over text.

He looked like he would have a sexy, velvety voice. That had always been a turn-on for her. Staci didn't go to sleep for another hour and, instead, studied his profile like she was trying to get an "A" on an exam. She wanted to know as much as she could so she wouldn't ask him any questions that had been answered on his profile.

Only his first name was on the dating profile so she wouldn't be able to search for him on social media, but she tried anyway. There were hundreds of Marcuses, but not her Marcus.

Later in her search, on the bottom right corner of his online profile, she saw that he had his social media profile linked. It was like she found gold.

On one of his profiles, he had the same pictures she already saw. He posted a lot of Bible verses and appeared to be very active in church. Every other picture was of him shaking the hand of some popular pastor or elder. He was definitely a social climber in the church, but she realized that she had been one as well. It was just that her social climbing experience ended with her becoming a pastor.

Staci closed her eyes and let her mind drift into all types of possibilities. This was probably her husband right in front of her. This was probably the man God had sent to be the help she needed by her side. She could feel it.

She said a silent prayer while still in bed and hoped to dream of the life she hoped they'd share together.

In the morning, Staci turned on her coffee maker and played soft music in the background while she picked out her clothes for the day. She was going to be interviewed by one of the local radio stations to promote her latest book, *Feminine Wisdom in the Name of Jesus*. It was a devotional as well as inspirational quotes for women who were improving their Christian walk.

However, this morning looked even brighter because she was going to get the chance to call Marcus. She didn't want to seem too desperate and call him first, but her fingers were itching to get him on the phone.

At 9:10, Staci found his name in her cellphone's address book and held her breath.

"Hello?" Marcus answered in a velvety baritone.

Staci was taken by surprise by how well his voice matched his pictures.

"Marcus?"

"Yes, this is he. How are you doing, sweetheart?"

Staci felt the butterflies in her chest rise and fall.

"I'm doing well. I'm just making some coffee. I'm about to get ready to go soon."

"What are you up to today?" he asked.

"I have a radio show to do today."

"Oh, big time, huh?"

"Not really. It's for a segment that features different religious leaders in the area. I'm promoting my book."

"And you write, too? Well, thank God I answered that message."

Staci chuckled.

"What are you up to today?" she asked.

"Oh, I'm supposed to be meeting with a group of ministers today to talk about this prayer line we're starting. We wanted to do something with social media where people can just pop up and ask for prayer. We're still figuring it out."

"That sounds nice. I see you're busy working on

projects."

"Oh, well yes. I keep myself busy. God is good. When was I going to get a chance to talk to you in person?"

"Like meeting somewhere?"

"Yeah. We could meet somewhere. Hopefully, this isn't too fast. I just wanted to see those pictures in motion."

Staci was impressed that he asked to meet up before using *FaceTime*.

"Would this be a date?" she asked, taking a sip of her coffee.

"Well, of course. I wouldn't mind this being our first official date. What type of food do you like?"

"I'm open to pretty much anything."

"How about steak?"

"A steak dinner?"

"Yeah, at *Schwartz Steak* in Malibu."

Staci hadn't been to a fancy restaurant in years. The fanciest restaurant she had visited in the last year was an upscale burger joint.

"Oh, well I guess I'll have to dress up."

"Could I come get you, or you would rather drive?"

Staci knew that rule number one was to never get in the car with a strange man, but she didn't get any weird vibes from him. Besides, she would just text her license plate number and the color of his car to Martha.

She was convinced that Marcus had to be the last of his kind, so she had to take a risk or risk never meeting a man of his caliber again.

"Yes, you can come get me. When?"

"Friday at six?"

"That sounds good."

"Well I'll let you go. I hope your interview goes well. I'll be praying for you. Text me when it's over. I'd love to hear about it, sweetheart."

Staci was smiling from ear to ear, gliding around her kitchen like Marcus was physically sweeping her off her feet. She couldn't wait to touch his solid biceps and be fully absorbed into his hug. His lips looked smooth and kissable. Staci couldn't believe that this was the man that God had waited for her to have. She always wanted a good man, but Marcus was more than she could have dreamt up herself.

An hour later, Staci still couldn't get Marcus out of her head. She looked at the pictures on his profile once again, and now they felt more real to her. The way he spoke to her on the phone made it seem like those pictures were no longer just a fantasy. He was a real person with a beautiful voice that wanted her. Marcus wanted her.

Nonetheless, he still didn't know she was a pastor.

Friday came, and Staci was still debating whether or not she wore the right outfit. She bought a pink dress that reached down to her knees. It had thick straps and a scoop neck that didn't reveal too much. Her freshly curled hair reached her shoulders, and a hint of her favorite Coco Chanel perfume wafted from her shoulders. She put on heels, but avoided putting on the highest ones she could find because she wanted to be comfortable. A small jacket to cover her arms felt tight, but she refused to have her arms bare.

Marcus texted her that he was on his way. Staci felt a couple beads of sweat fall down the sides of her body. She rushed to the bathroom to reapply her deodorant.

Marcus arrived within three minutes.

She heard him pull his car into her driveway and then walk toward the door.

Staci opened her door after the third knock. His imposing figure greeted her at the door. His white teeth were brilliant and a small, gold earring shimmered in his right ear. Staci loved how his beard brushed across her face as they hugged. It wasn't a tight hug, but it was enough for her to inhale his cologne. It smelled like a musky rain, as if he just hopped out the shower.

"You look beautiful tonight. Lookin' like a First Lady!"

Staci grabbed his arm and allowed him to lead her to the car. He drove a black Honda Civic. Staci stepped inside his car and sank into his leather-covered seats.

He turned on traditional Gospel hits from his phone and shivers crept down Staci's back every time he looked at her.

She was too nervous to start the conversation and, instead, checked her emails.

Eventually, Marcus observed something interesting on the street and then the conversation flowed like water. Staci felt like she was talking to an old friend. It was like they had known each other for years and were reconnecting.

Staci didn't even notice that they had reached Malibu. She could tell Marcus loved to have deep conversations and had a vast knowledge about a variety of topics. He knew everything, from church to travel.

Conversations with her peers in theology school were never nearly as interesting.

The valet met them at the entrance of the restaurant. Marcus let Staci hold onto his arm as they walked in together. The hostess seated them within five minutes.

A candlelit table was set up by the large windows that overlooked the ocean. It was one of the most romantic scenes Staci had ever witnessed. She felt like she was in a movie.

Marcus ordered ice water and warm sourdough bread to get them started.

"So, how do you like this place?"

"It's beautiful. You really outdid yourself."

"So, why don't you tell me a little bit more about yourself? You gonna have me staring at you all night like some school boy," he said jokingly.

"Well, I am earning my Doctorate of Theology at the Baker's University in the valley."

"Oh, really? I have a close cousin that went there."

"You said you were earning your elder's license?"

"Yes, I am. I'm still trying to get more speaking engagements so I can get even better at what I do. I'm trying to get a larger following online as well. Do you travel around?"

Staci's heart began beating quickly. "No."

"Where do you speak?"

"Well, I actually preach."

"Where?"

"Center of Praise. I'm the pastor."

"Pastor? In the Church of God in Christ? They never had female pastors."

"Well, I'm the first one. I was ordained by the jurisdictional bishop. They lost their pastor about a year ago."

"Wow, well I've met quite a few female ministers, but I've never met one with their own church."

"Well, you're looking at her."

The waiter came by to take their order. Staci was glad that she got to get the attention off herself for a second while they both ordered a medium-well steak.

"So, a pastor?" Marcus said with one eyebrow raised.

"Does that make you uncomfortable?"

"Oh no! Not at all! That's a wonderful accomplishment for anyone, and not just a woman. I just would have never thought that a woman as beautiful as you would be in that type of position. That's an honor. I bet you can preach with the best of them, huh?"

Staci nervously pushed back a lock of her hair next to her chin and smiled. "Well, I do pretty well. At first, my membership wasn't too fond of me, but they've grown to like me."

"How long have you been COGIC?" he asked.

"All my life."

"Do you ever have time to have hobbies outside the church?" he asked, looking around for the waiter to refill his glass of water.

"Well, not really. Being a pastor is truly a full-time job. I barely have time for anything else. I mean, I have time to date, but I can't just get up and go when I want to. I do plan on doing more traveling out of the state to preach."

"Do you have any videos of you preaching?" Marcus asked.

"Well, I have a few on social media, but I'm not active on there like that."

"You should really look into it. I have over ten thousand followers now. You have to reach the people however you can. Actually, I've been thinking about doing a virtual church because I think that's where the future is with preaching. All these young people are on their phones now, but we still got to reach them."

"I agree, but I have been working very closely with the youth lately and I found out that many of them don't mind coming to church. It's just that they want to be able to do something more than just sit there. They want to be involved. I actually just developed a praise dance team and am working on getting a youth choir together."

Staci watched Marcus' eyes get wider with every sentence.

"You're a very ambitious woman. You don't meet too many like you. I really like that. A lot of women out there are looking for what a man can do for them, but they should have their own."

Their steaks came to the table. Staci and Marcus ate in silence for a few minutes.

With his mouth full, Marcus started the conversation again. "So, how long had you been on the website? Have you met anyone else?"

"No, I was wondering the same thing about you."

"I really haven't met anyone that I had a lot in

common with. A lot of women think that it's weird that I never married. Sometimes, men don't always find 'the one.' I never wanted to start a relationship with a woman for the sake of it. I intend to be with one woman, be faithful to her, have a family, and live in the body of Christ."

"That's also what I desire. I want a man who works hard and wants to uplift me and my future children."

Staci remembered that she hadn't asked Marcus what he did for a living outside of the ministry. She didn't want to be too invasive, but she was also wary of dating someone that was technically unemployed. However, Marcus was such a good man that she was afraid of ruining the vibe by asking him key questions about his background.

She started with the basics.

"Do you have a good relationship with your parents?"

"Yes."

"Where did you go to school?"

"I went to Brigham University for a while."

Staci thought that was an odd answer, but she didn't think that a degree made a man a better person.

"What kind of work do you do during the week?"

Marcus started coughing and then took a sip of water. "I actually drive for a ride share company and then do delivery work. I really like my job. It allows me to move around and not stay in one place. I never liked the office life. Besides, I'm trying to work on my app for prayer and develop a church either online or offline. I want to work from the ground up. I'm not interested in inheriting other people's members. No offense, it's just that, like you mentioned, it can take people a while to get used to you."

"Yeah, it does. It wasn't the easiest situation, but I truly love Center of Praise and I'm glad that I was placed there. Have you ever dated someone in the ministry?" she asked.

"No, I haven't. This is the first time."

"How do you feel about it?"

"I don't mind it at all. Now, I've been used to women taking other ministerial positions in church instead of becoming a pastor. But, this is a new day and age. Women should be able to take any position in the church."

Staci felt the muscles in her body relax. Her biggest fear was Marcus not being able to accept that she was the pastor of not only a church, but one of the largest churches in South Los Angeles.

They talked back and forth for two hours. They shared laughs and then they began reflecting on some of the Bible verses they had read recently.

"Do you think we'd be able to do this again?" Marcus asked. "I had such a good time. It was a lovely evening being here with you."

"I had a wonderful time. I'd love to see you again."

"You want to head back to my place or yours and relax for a bit before we go home?"

Staci really wanted to continue the night with him, but she was not going to visit his home under any circumstances. She didn't want him to come over her house either.

"Um, how about we just schedule another date soon? I don't think we know each other well enough to see each other at each others' homes."

"That's perfectly fine. It was just a suggestion. We

don't have to. I didn't mean to make you feel uncomfortable."

"You don't make me feel uncomfortable. I had a wonderful time with you and would love to continue it."

Staci was a virgin and wanted to keep it that way until she married. Although she had had temptation more than once, she knew that it was better to be married than to risk having her heart broken.

"I'll take you home, sweetheart. How about this Monday afternoon at four?"

Staci checked her calendar on her phone and then looked up with a smile.

"Yes. I'd love that. I really would."

Chapter 4

Safe and Sound

Staci and Marcus began getting closer as the weeks went on. She talked to him on the phone every night. Staci felt like this was the best friend she had been missing for years. He prayed with her. They read the Bible together and even sent each other inspirational verses. Marcus always had a listening ear when she was feeling down and knew just the right words to say to support her when church members were acting up and the deacon board was putting pressure on her.

He became her rock. Staci began to talk to him more than anyone else. She had begun to contact her parents no more than once a month. Martha had even wondered why Staci seemed so distant lately.

Pastor? Were you still coming to the Music Department meeting? You didn't respond to the group text, Martha texted.

Staci reached over to pick up her phone. She and Marcus were enjoying a walk by the ocean in Manhattan Beach. She loved that he knew how to pick out the most romantic, yet cheap outings. Staci didn't ask for much. She just wanted his time.

Yet, having gotten so caught up in their whirlwind romance, Staci had forgotten about the Music Department meeting that evening. She never missed a meeting for any department. It was important to her to make sure that she supported every aspect of the church. It was hard work, but she didn't want to be out of reach.

"Marcus, I forgot I was supposed to go to the department meeting tonight? I don't know how that slipped my mind."

He held her hand as they walked up the steep,

sandy stairs near the beach home. "Can't you tell them that you'll make it next time? I don't want to get you in trouble."

"No. I'll go. I don't like missing meetings."

"Well, you are just *some* kind of woman. Boss lady, huh?"

Staci smirked. "I'm just the pastor. Nothing out of the ordinary. Being a pastor may seem glamorous to some people, but it's work."

"Well luckily, I get to be the man right by your side."

Staci began texting several people that she would be at the meeting late, but to start without her.

Staci asked if they could sit down for a few minutes. Marcus agreed.

He began fiddling with his phone, and Staci saw that he appeared angry about something.

"What's wrong, Marcus?"

"Oh, it's just my business partners. We're trying to get this app off the ground and they're trippin'."

"What are you trying to do?"

"Well, first we need an investor. We have to hire an app developer and everybody is talking all over the place. I don't know what they want to do. Right now, we need an investor. We need someone that believes in the vision."

"Have your business partners contributed?"

"Yeah, they have. It's just that I been working like a dog lately and these bills been crazy. I thought I would have enough to put in."

"Well, I believe in your vision. I think a prayer app is a wonderful idea. The way the world is so fast paced now, we need something like that. It's a great idea. You shouldn't give up."

Marcus shrugged and kept texting.

"How much money is it going to cost to get a developer? Is that the person who will actually make the app?"

"Yeah, they'll make the app. It's too much money, though."

Staci placed her hand on his and looked into his eyes. She felt like he was on the brink of tears.

"Marcus, how much is it?"

"They said they want a one thousand dollar down

payment before they start."

Staci breathed in.

"It's okay. Can I write you a check?"

"No, Staci baby. You don't have to do that?"

"No. I really want to support you. However, I need to know something before I move on."

"What?" he asked with his eyes widened.

"I want to know what we are. Are we just friends or in a relationship? I know it's been just a month, but I'd like to know."

Staci knew that was the question that ran most men away, but she was determined to finally get in the relationship she had been dreaming about for years.

"You're my woman."

"As in?"

"As in my girlfriend. I'm in a relationship with you. I care about you."

Marcus kissed her softly on the forehead. He then brought her lips toward his and gave her a smooth peck. Staci felt her electricity race through her body.

"Does this mean you'll finally introduce me to the church?"

"Well. I don't encourage non-marriage relationships, but you know we're going to have to say that we're *friends*."

"I know the COGIC way. I know not to go around saying girlfriend and boyfriend."

Marcus stood up to dust off his jeans. He grabbed her hand so it interlocked with his and they began walking toward his car.

"Now, you know I don't plan on being anybody's girlfriend for too long. I just want to make that clear."

Staci crossed her arms over her chest and raised an eyebrow. Marcus held onto her shoulders and looked into her eyes. "Baby, I have nothing but the best planned for us. I want you to know that I want marriage, kids, everything. You won't have to worry."

In the car, Staci sent money to Marcus over an app that sends cash to another user. A single, sharp tone echoed from Marcus' phone. He had received the money.

"You got it, baby?" Staci asked.

"Yup," Marcus said, looking at his phone. "Thank you, baby. I really appreciate it. You didn't have to."

❖

On Friday night, Staci decided to meet with Marcus once again. He invited her to go to a free music show in Downtown L.A.

Staci didn't like to attend too many non-Gospel events, but she made an exception. There was going to be a Gospel artist featured toward the end.

Marcus and Staci huddled on a bench about twenty feet away from the concert. It was chilly, so she brought a blanket for the two of them to share. She laid her head on his shoulder and allowed her body to melt into his while he whispered sweet nothings in her ear.

After thirty minutes into the show, Marcus appeared to be getting bored. He began scrolling down his phone, and Staci peaked over to see what he was doing.

The Christian dating app was still on his phone. He had lowered the backlight so no one would be able to clearly see what he was doing. Staci pretended that she wanted to see the concert better and leaned onto his shoulder. Her eyes grazed over his phone.

She gasped.

He had just clicked out of the app because she recognized the icon. It was the same Christian dating app that they had met on.

"Marcus! What are you doing?"

"What?" He immediately put his phone in his pocket.

"You were on that app. I saw you."

Staci shook her head and moved a few inches away from Marcus. She couldn't bear to look at him anymore.

"On what?"

"I recognized it, Marcus. We haven't been together one month and you're already on the search for somebody else."

"Somebody else? I wasn't on it."

"I clearly saw it, Marcus. That's the app. We met on it. I used to have it on my phone, too, but I took it off when we began to get more serious."

Staci had erased the app the day after she went on her date with Marcus.

"Baby, I'm not on it. I probably forgot to take it off my phone, but I'm not using it."

"I saw you close out of it."

"No, that's not what happened. I would never go on it. I wouldn't go on a dating app with you sitting right here."

Staci knew what she saw, but she didn't want to argue anymore.

"Staci, you really think I would go on some app?"

"Take it off your phone now," Staci said sternly.

"I'll take it off when I get home. I promise. I was actually trying to hold on to some of our first conversations. I didn't know it would bother you like that. I don't really erase any apps I put on my phone. I'm kind of bad with that. I have some games on my phone that I haven't played in a minute."

Marcus pulled Staci toward him and kissed her on the forehead. "I'm sorry, baby. I didn't mean to upset you."

His big hands pulled her in so she could sit between his legs. Her head sank into his chest. Staci felt like a little girl on Santa's lap.

"I just don't want anything to come between us. I really like you. You make me feel like the woman I was meant to be. I'm not Pastor Bernard with you. I'm just Staci. I like that, and I want to keep it that way."

"Baby, I'll always be here for you. I'm going to keep it that way."

Staci focused on the concert again. Marcus wrapped his arms around her to keep her warm. She wished he could be with her all the time.

"Would you come to church on Sunday? I think I'm ready," she whispered.

"Yeah. I'd love to. I wouldn't mind getting to see my baby preach."

For the rest of the night, she couldn't stop looking into his eyes and fantasizing about the wedding she knew they'd have soon. White flowers, a long train, and hopefully officiated by the jurisdictional bishop.

She wanted everything, as long as she had him.

❖

Staci refused to let Marcus stay overnight at her house, but it felt like they lived together because she was on the phone with him as early as 6 A.M. some mornings. They would begin their day by praying together and then catching up on what happened the previous day. Marcus always had interesting stories about his deliveries, but Staci usually took up most of the time talking about everything that was going on at church.

Sunday morning was like any other. She dressed in a white suit because it was communion day. A white hat with tulle partially hid her face, and a gold brooch in the shape of a cross gave her outfit a pop of color. Her suits always had the skirt below the knee, but she decided to move it up at exactly knee length. She didn't think anyone at church would notice.

That Sunday morning was the prettiest she had felt in a while. She always had good self-esteem, but being in love with Marcus gave her an extra pep in her step.

With her Bible in hand, she pulled out of her driveway. Congregational Gospel songs played in her speakers while she sang along.

Take the Lord along with you everywhere you go!
Take the Lord along with you everywhere you go!

She was one of the first people to arrive at Center of Praise. Deacon Johnson and Deacon Brown had unlocked the church, so Staci was able to walk in. She texted Marcus to see when he would arrive. She told him he didn't have to come too early. She wanted him to make his appearance around 11 A.M.

She slipped into her office before Sunday school

started and prayed for the service as well as Marcus' safe arrival.

One of the youth ministers wanted to have a short meeting with her during Sunday school, so she placed Deacon Johnson in charge of the adult and children's Sunday school classes.

Staci ended up not attending Sunday school. She got caught up texting Marcus, who said he was on his way. She sent him a picture of what she looked like and then texted him.

Ready to see you! Praise God!

He didn't respond right away, but Martha knocked on her door before she began to get too anxious about not receiving an immediate response.

"Pastor? I think service is ready to start. They sent me back here to come get you."

"I'll be right there, Martha."

Staci grabbed her Bible and clutched it, along with her purse. The click-clack of her heels made an echo throughout the dark hallway. Each second, she felt her feet moving more quickly. She had to stop herself from almost running.

Once she entered the auditorium, the praise and worship team had begun singing to get the membership warmed up.

Todd greeted her with a head nod once she walked in and she nodded back. She wondered if he always wanted to get her attention because he wanted a raise. Staci was not ready to increase anyone's salary until the membership became larger.

Testimony service continued, and then the first offering for the sick and the shut-in. Staci kept watching the doors of the church. Each time it opened, her heart dropped. By default, she smiled at her faithful members that were coming in late. The anxiety from waiting was beginning to frustrate her. It was a faux pas for a pastor to check their phone while in the pulpit, but she couldn't help herself and reached for her purse under her chair.

Almost as soon as she raised her head with her phone in her hand, Marcus entered the building. The ushers, who were always surprised by visitors, offered him a program and directed him to one of the open spaces in the middle pews.

Staci stood up and began clapping her hands to the music. She got his attention within seconds.

Marcus also got everyone else's attention. Staci saw Martha elbow one of the sopranos in the choir as soon as she saw Marcus take a seat.

Other women noticed him and, before long, he had all the single women locked in on the most masculine energy in the church.

The married women couldn't keep their eyes off him either. Sister Keneisha's husband pulled her hand to sit down during the song once he saw his wife gaze too long at the mystery man.

Staci didn't like how he garnered all this attention, but he was an attractive man so her jealousy eventually faded into pride.

Following communion, Staci delayed benediction to allow Marcus to have a few words.

"Church, this here is one of the most profound ministers of our generation. This man sure can preach. I'm not going to let him loose today, but you will see him very soon. Please welcome my friend, Minister Marcus Vincent!"

Marcus stood and walked toward the pulpit. He

stood at the podium first, but Staci welcomed him to the pulpit to speak with her microphone.

The church was already enchanted with him and he hadn't even said a word. He had a natural charm about him that even made the deacons swoon.

"Center of Praise, I hope this won't be my last visit. I can tell God has been blessing this beautiful church. Thank you to my friend, Pastor Bernard, for that lovely welcome. I plan on doing what God has led me to do. A long time ago, an old man told me that change is good. God thrives in change. When we stay the same, we can't become closer to him. Come Sunday, I hope your pastor will let me say a few more words."

A wave of clapping and cheering followed.

Staci didn't mean to allow Marcus to preach so soon, but she was impressed with how well the church gravitated toward him. She nodded her head and pulled up her phone's calendar.

Marcus bringing the message.

She wrote it down, winked at Marcus, and watched him smoothly walk back to his seat like he floated out of her imagination right into her reality.

Following a meeting about the church's finances, Staci raced home to freshen up for their meeting with her parents. They lived seventy miles away, so it would take the couple at least two hours to get out there.

Staci was excited because this was the first person that she had ever introduced to her parents. They had been looking for her to bring someone home for years. She never wanted to bring anyone that she felt would be a short-term fling, but things had been going so well with Marcus. They had been dating for a little over a month, but

130

it felt like they had been together for years.

He finished her sentences and always had the right Bible verse she needed for every situation.

Her mother was supposed to cook dinner. Staci hadn't had her mother's home cooking for years and was excited to come home and spend some time with them. She used to love spending time with her parents but since she moved out on her own and then became responsible for a church, there was little time left for anyone other than the most pressing matters at the Center of Praise.

Twenty minutes before Marcus was supposed to pick her up, she heard her phone ring.

It was Marcus.

"Hello, baby. How are you doing?"

"I'm doing fine. Are you still coming by?"

"Well, see that's why I called. I'm supposed to preach at a church tonight because the pastor couldn't make it."

Staci cut him off.

"So, you thought it would be best to cancel on my family dinner just to go preach?"

"Sweetheart, you don't understand. I know you do this for a living, but I rarely get opportunities to preach these days."

"I'm giving you an opportunity at my church."

"Yes. You said you would let me say a few words one Sunday. I'm trying to make this my career and I can't turn down too many opportunities. This is part of my bread and butter."

"So, being a pastor is just a job to you?" Staci asked. She was trying not to raise her voice.

"No. However, I may get a little money from this. Anything helps. I'm not the pastor of a large church like you full-time. I'm trying to get there."

"Marcus, no one else can replace you? I really expected you to come tonight."

"Well, I need as much practice behind the pulpit as I can."

"How about you guest preach for me once or twice a month? I'd also like you to be part of my Sunday evening services, where I invite pastors from other churches and cities. Would that be okay?"

"Yes. I could do that. I wouldn't mind getting that practice in."

"You're still going to go tonight?" Staci asked.

"I think I can get someone to do it instead of me. I'll just come right now and I'll let them know."

"You're coming to pick me up?"

"Yes."

Staci relaxed her shoulders and breathed out. "Alright. I'll see you soon. Dress comfortably. It's going to be a long ride. It'll take two hours to get there."

"Can I just drive halfway and you do the other half? My business partners will be texting me and I want to be available."

"Um, sure."

Staci sent a text to Martha, who had become her unofficial personal assistant.

Martha, put Marcus Vincent down as the speaker for next Sunday.

Who?

Marcus Vincent. You know, the man that came out this Sunday? Put him down for this Sunday and fifth Sunday. I want him to preach.

I meant to ask you. How do you know him, Pastor? Martha asked.

He's my very good friend. I wanted to give him some exposure. He's a very good preacher.

That's the one you had been telling me about earlier? Was that the one that is trying to get his prayer app off the ground? You met him on the dating site I told you about?

Yes. He's the one, Staci said with a beaming smile

135

on her face.

Well. I would still wait it out and get to know him more. He seems nice, though.

He is. He's a wonderful man.

Minutes later, Marcus arrived at her house to pick him up. She wore a sweat suit, but her make-up was still on and she wore her hair down.

I'll see you on Wednesday at the church, Martha. Staci sent her last text for the day.

Marcus picked her up promptly, but asked if Staci could drive her car instead because his had been giving him problems.

"It's fine," she said, grabbing her keys.

Marcus was wearing a simple white t-shirt, jeans,

and a sports jacket. His new Nike tennis shoes looked like he had just taken them out of the box.

"Well, you look nice," Staci said, reaching up to give him a kiss. This time, they shared the most intimate kiss she had ever felt. She placed her hands around his neck and then pressed her body into his. She felt his penis get hard above her waist through his pants. Once she felt that, Staci pulled back.

"What's wrong?" he asked.

"I think we should get going. It's going to be a long drive."

Staci grabbed her purse and got inside her car. Marcus pushed his seat back and put his hands behind his head to relax. For most of the ride, he was busy on his phone while Staci fought the unintended Sunday evening traffic she encountered due to an accident.

She turned the music down so they could start talking to each other. "What you doing on that phone?"

"Nothing!" Marcus put his phone in pocket, as if he was startled.

"Why did you put it away? I just thought you were talking to your business partners."

"Oh yeah, I was. I was talking to my business partners. It's just that you scared me a little bit. I thought you hit something."

Staci raised her eyebrow and shook her hand, but kept driving for another thirty minutes until she tried to talk to Marcus again.

"So, I was thinking we should go on a short day trip together. I was thinking about going to Old Town Pasadena."

"Where all those rich people shop? Oh, I forgot. You got it like that," he teased.

"No, it's just that they have a lot of stores I like. It's okay, though. It doesn't sound like you want to go."

"I do. I want to go anywhere with my baby."

They had been in the car for an hour and Staci asked Marcus if he could take over the wheel because she was getting tired.

"Oh, do you think I could just drive back? I got a bunch of emails I'm trying to answer, baby."

"All of sudden?" Staci asked.

"Yeah. I'm just trying to get some business taken care of."

"I put you on the calendar for this Sunday and fifth

Sunday. I forgot to tell you."

"Really? Two Sundays? Thank you, baby!" Marcus reached over to kiss her on the forehead. "You don't know what this means. I'm gonna get so much more exposure."

"And you'll be a blessing to the people," she added.

"Oh, of course. Of course. God is still in the blessing business, and I'm here to spread the word."

"You know what you're going to preach about?"

"Well, I'm going to use one of the sermons I wrote a couple years ago. I call it, 'Put on The Whole Armor of God.'"

"That sounds beautiful. You should tell my father about it. I'm sure he could give you some pointers. He was training to be a pastor years ago. Now, he just preaches when he can."

"He never wanted a church?"

"He never wanted the responsibility of a church. I can understand. It's a lot to handle."

Marcus remained quiet for the remainder of the ride. Once they approached her parents' home, Staci sat in the car for a couple minutes in the driveway.

"You tired, baby?" Marcus asked.

"Yeah."

"I'll drive home. Don't worry."

The couple walked toward her parents' front porch and rang the doorbell. Her mother answered within seconds.

Staci squeezed her mother as hard as she could and then released her to kiss her dad on the cheek.

Marcus shook their hands and sat down on the nearest couch.

Staci introduced Marcus to her parents, Deborah and Eldridge, who appeared immediately impressed by him.

Marcus knew all the right words to say and had her parents enchanted within minutes. His parents also had southern roots, so he knew how to charm them.

"A preacher, huh?" Eldridge said. "I wouldn't mind having three preachers in the family one day."

"Oh, Eldridge," her mother sighed.

"Well, he's actually going to preach this Sunday and on the fifth Sunday."

"I'd love to see what you got, son," her father said, sipping coffee.

"Preaching is not my only thing," Marcus began.

"He does delivery service. He's a driver," Staci said, cutting him off.

Staci saw Marcus quickly roll his eyes before he began speaking louder. "Actually, I'm the CEO of my own company. I'm developing an app for virtual prayer. Just like people go on apps for therapy these days, I'm creating one where somebody can pick up their phone and request prayers from any of our ministers online. I think this is going to change the game for young Christians."

"Well, that sounds like a wonderful idea!" her mother exclaimed.

Staci loved when Marcus talked about his ideas, but she had never heard him say that he was CEO before.

With her, he was a delivery driver. With her family and the church, he was the owner of a potential multi-million dollar business.

"I expect it to make at least one million in the first two years with advertisements, and then I'll charge those that want counseling. I'm even think of creating merchandise. My business partners and I are always coming up with something."

Staci thought to herself that she had never met his business partners, but he was so busy with them all the time; she didn't think he would ever have time to introduce her.

Staci's mother walked toward the kitchen to turn the stove off. Everyone followed her in because they knew the food would be ready soon. They each took their seats.

"You know, Staci makes me so proud. She is the first woman to become a pastor in the Church of God in

Christ. I thought I would never see the day. She was always so ambitious. If you heard her preach, you'd see why the bishop chose her."

Staci was beaming with pride. Her father's eyes were glassy with tears. He stood up to kiss her on the forehead before he went to the cabinet to take out the plates.

Staci looked over at Marcus, who took his phone out and didn't add to the conversation. Staci could feel he was irritated, but she assumed it was because no one liked to hear someone's parents bragging out their child.

"What you got to eat, Mother Bernard?" Marcus asked, finally looking up from his phone.

"Oh, I put some greens on the stove. I got some cornbread. There's some macaroni and cheese in there."

"Well you done outdid yourself, mother." Marcus

joked. "Now, it looks like you preach with the stove. I love the traditional woman that cooks and keeps the home clean. Did I tell you, you sure do know how to keep a nice house? It's beautiful here."

Staci suddenly felt thirsty and went to get some water from the refrigerator.

"Thank you, son. I appreciate it."

"If you ask me, I know that women can do a lot these days, but it's beautiful when a woman can contribute to the household with more than just money."

"I know that's right!" Eldridge interjected.

Staci began to feel her face flush with heat. He had always seemed supportive of her career choice but suddenly, he wanted her to cook. She hadn't cooked for him yet because she wasn't comfortable with a man coming over to her home yet. She felt that it would lead to temptation.

Following dinner, her parents retired into the living room to watch the Christian TV channel. Marcus and Staci sat on the porch outside. Staci made herself a bowl of ice cream to take with her. Marcus grabbed a glass of lemonade.

"What was that about in there?" Staci asked.

"About what?"

"About me not cooking? I thought you didn't mind that. You know it's too early for us to be going over to each other's house. I also didn't know that you wanted me to do that."

"No, it's not that. I admire a strong woman like you. But I'm a man. I would like a little home cooking sometimes. We don't have to rush, though."

Staci felt a tear come to her eye. She hid it by moving her head to the side and looking in another direction.

"I guess I just thought that you liked things the way they are. I didn't know this was some kind of competition. I don't like you pitting me against my mom."

"No one is pitting you against your mother. I just have a vision of a happy family one day. I know you can cook. I never said you couldn't."

Staci actually couldn't. She was always so busy in college and traveling around the world that she never had time to learn. She knew how to make a few things to eat, but mostly ate out because she was always busy. Marcus had hit a sensitive spot. Apparently, she wasn't the most feminine woman in the world.

"Staci, I know you aren't about to sit up here and think about that all night long. I do love you. If I didn't like someone like you in your position, I wouldn't be in a relationship with you."

Staci didn't say much for the rest of the evening.

"Now, we should start heading back. I want to get started on my sermon. Do you mind driving? I'm going to hold a conference call with my COO and CFO," Marcus said.

"You can't do that while driving?"

"Yes, but I need to be focused."

Staci sighed and nodded.

"Yes. I'll drive Marcus. I don't think the traffic going back will be as bad."

Chapter 5

Love Lies

While scrolling online looking for deals following a long meeting she had with a few of the church officials, Staci came across a beautiful gold watch that was on sale.

It was for men and reminded her of the luxury watches she sometimes saw in the window. It had a band that somewhat resembled the Rolex. It had been discounted by more than forty percent. She had seen the ad for the website on social media and clicked on it to hopefully find some new jewelry. Staci loved brooches and watches.

She thought of getting the watch for her dad, but Marcus' birthday was coming up. She wanted to surprise him with the watch and take him out to dinner.

Her birthday was one week after his, so she planned to take him out a few days before his birthday so his plans wouldn't get mixed up with hers. Staci purchased the watch and tried to get the fastest shipping possible. She planned for it to be on her doorstep by tomorrow.

Church business had been overwhelming lately, but she was excited to spend some more time with Marcus while she could. She booked the restaurant she would take him to in advance. It was a steakhouse in Beverly Hills. Staci wanted to get a luxury car to take them there, but she would have to see how much money she had in the next couple of days.

So far, Staci had been improving the finances of the church. Center of Praise had increased the money in its savings account. The accounts for hospitality, the youth department, the usher department, and the women's department were growing. Staci believed in being frugal, but not cheap. The former pastor, Bishop Mattison, rarely liked to spend money on large events, but Staci found a way to make sure that each event that was held was reinvested in the church. Her vision for the Center of Praise was to develop a homeless shelter, a retirement home, and even a preschool for the local residents.

Lately, Marcus had been asking for more help for his business. They had argued back and forth about it, but Staci remained unmoved. She wanted to help him, but she planned to help him more if he was her husband. She never said that to him, but she didn't want Marcus getting too comfortable getting money from her. She wanted a bigger commitment.

Staci had hinted to Martha that she felt that Marcus would propose on her birthday one Sunday afternoon while she was straightening up the pulpit. Martha was typing away on her laptop in the choir stand.

"You really think so? What makes you think he's going to do it this time?"

"I don't know, but I have a feeling that he's thinking about it more. We had the marriage talk again yesterday. He says he's ready but just wants to get his business off the ground more. I told him that he didn't need to do that. He told me that I was right and that he shouldn't wait around. He said he wanted to get to the next step as soon as possible."

Martha closed her laptop. "When do you think he's going to do it?"

"To be honest, I think he's going to propose on my birthday. He took me to a jewelry store and allowed me to pick out a few rings I liked. I told him that I'm not picky."

"He's supposed to bring the message this coming Sunday, right?"

"He is. Our birthdays are almost here, too. I bought him a beautiful watch. I think he's going to love it."

"Well, as long as he puts that much thought into your gift."

"What do you mean?" Staci asked.

"It's just that you're such a giving person, Pastor. I don't want anyone to take advantage of that."

"Marcus? Oh no, he would never. He's a sweetheart. Besides, he gives me what I really need. He's there for support, for prayer, and when I just need someone to talk to. Those things are priceless."

Martha shrugged her shoulders and began putting her laptop away.

Staci grabbed her own laptop bag and Bible. When she grabbed her phone, she sent a text to Marcus.

I'll talk to you tonight. You're still available Saturday night?

Yeah. Of course. Talk to you soon he replied.

❖

The day of Marcus' birthday, Staci drove him to Tao's Steakhouse in Beverly Hills. She wore a long evening gown with a higher split than she was used to. Her heels sparkled and her hair was twisted in a simple updo. The watch she had to present to Marcus was in her purse.

The ride over was mostly silent, but Staci had gotten used to it. For some reason, he was more talkative over the phone. In person, he was the busiest man alive. However, Staci believed in him. She didn't want to get in the way of his start-up business.

Instead, she attempted to start a conversation about what he was working on. Conversations about Center of Praise tended to lead back to whatever Marcus was into at the time.

"Are you excited?" Staci asked, making a left turn.

"Excited about what?" Marcus asked.

"Your birthday. This is also our first evening out in a long time. The next time we'll get to see each other is at church."

"Yeah. It's exciting. I'm sorry, I'm just distracted. The company I'm working for is sending me all these emails. I guess I'm going to have to go to the warehouse tomorrow morning and collect some packages. My business partner, Michael, said he knows someone that can possibly get us an office downtown so we can all work together at once. I'm trying to do this full time and I think I'm really close."

"Well, I believe in you, baby. You'll get there. When I was trying to become a pastor, I had to go through a lot. It's not easy. Being a woman didn't make it any better either."

Marcus kept his eyes glued to his phone.

Staci arrived at their destination within twenty-five minutes of picking him up. Since she had reservations, they were seated within minutes.

Marcus ordered the filet mignon and lobster. He also wanted to get a taste of one of the most expensive wines the restaurant had to offer.

Staci decided to get pasta and a side salad. She wasn't the biggest fan of steak but knew Marcus liked it.

He softly grabbed her hand and then rubbed her thumb with his. Staci loved when he treated her tenderly in public. Marcus told her how much he loved her and then grabbed the back of her hand to kiss it.

Once they were done eating, Staci took the watch out of her purse and presented it to Marcus. The light reflected against the gold and made Marcus turn his head away for a second to get the brightness out of his eyes.

"That's so beautiful, baby. That's so beautiful!" He gasped.

He put it on and began gently touching the band and the face of the watch.

"It's not a Rolex but it's beautiful and regal. I couldn't help myself."

Marcus then reached into his pocket to get something out. Staci felt her heart start racing so quickly, she felt a little lightheaded.

"Yes, Marcus?"

It was a tiny ring box that looked much smaller in his large hands. He opened it, and inside was a plain silver band with a rose etched onto the front.

"This is a promise ring, baby. I wanted to let you know that I can't wait to be your husband one day."

"Oh. It's beautiful," she lied. Staci put it on and tried her best to hide her shame from the other patrons who must have thought it was a proposal. She put her hands underneath the table.

"Oh, and do you mind if this counts as your birthday dinner, too? I'll pay half."

"You'll be busy on my birthday?"

"I'm supposed to go up to Oakland to preach. I forgot to tell you. I had planned this a while back. I can take you out after, though. I'll just be up there for like two days. Is that cool?"

"Yeah. It's fine." Staci felt out of breath and confused at the same time.

"You didn't like this ring?" Marcus asked.

"No. No, I loved the ring. It's beautiful."

"You know we're going to get married soon, right? Is that what you're worried about?"

"No. Not at all. I just didn't expect to give each other presents tonight."

"Yeah, well thankfully, both our birthdays are right next to each other so we can celebrate at the same time. Isn't that nice?"

Staci felt a tear form in her right eye, but she grabbed a napkin and pretended she had to cough and quickly wiped her face. She had put so much effort into taking him to a gorgeous restaurant and purchasing an expensive watch, and he decided to give her a promise ring and pay half for the meal because he couldn't go out for her birthday.

"I'm a little upset that I won't see you on my birthday."

"But, Staci. I'm here now. You don't have to worry. This was a great idea. We can just celebrate at the same time. This is a beautiful watch, by the way."

"Thank you. This ring looks really nice, too. I'll just have to get it sized."

Staci then felt a rush of sadness run through her. She had been expecting so much of Marcus when he was just trying to get by with what he had. He didn't have as much money as she did and was still trying to chase his dream of working in the ministry full-time. He didn't have access to what she had access to every day. Marcus had done his best, and she knew she should be grateful instead of worrying about a ring.

She had faith he would propose soon. Besides, he was a man who had never been married and had no children, so Staci was sure that starting a family was very new to him.

The waiter came by and placed dessert menus on each side of the table. Staci gave hers back, but Marcus ordered right away. He wanted a crème brûlée with a side of chocolate truffles.

"You don't want any ice cream or nothing?" Marcus asked.

"No. I'm fine. I'm perfectly fine. I don't have that much of a sweet tooth right now."

Marcus discussed what he planned on preaching about on Sunday. He wanted to use some props to illustrate his point.

"Do you have a chess and checkers board lying around? I'm thinking about including those into my message."

"Yes. I do. We have them in the Sunday school room. The kids sometimes come by for our afterschool program."

"You have an afterschool program now? It's free?"

"No. However, it can be subsidized for those that use social services such as EBT. Most of our parents pay. It's not that much and we have such great teachers and activities. Sometimes, our kids go on fieldtrips. It's been such a nice addition to our church."

"So you're just rolling in the dough, huh?" Marcus laughed.

"I wouldn't necessarily say that. All the money we bring in helps to support our church."

"You get a salary, right?" Marcus asked.

"Yes, but it doesn't come from the after school

program. However, I have a salary and so does my music department. My youth department chairlady and the deacons that have been there the longest are also on payroll."

"Wow. That's good. I didn't think that little church in Watts had it going on like that."

"Well, it does and we're expanding. It's not the easiest, but advertising online has helped us bring in some new members."

"You can count me as one of your newest members. I plan on coming every Sunday I'm not traveling. I want to be where the spirit of God is in the midst."

Staci felt relaxed again. "Yes, well you know we're in the business of getting folks saved. We just prayed the demon of drug abuse off a young man a month ago. We just got the praise report from him that he hasn't put a prescription drug in his mouth since he set foot in our church."

"You have a lot of outreach programs, right? Those have really been getting you noticed on social media, right?"

"Well, I'm not sure about that because I have a social media manager. I don't run my own pages. I only write statuses every now and then. I never post pictures. I leave that up to the photographer."

"Right." Marcus' voice trailed off. Staci saw that his facial expressions no longer seemed interested in continuing with the conversation.

The waiter came back with their bill.

Staci immediately put her purse on the table to take her wallet out. Marcus didn't move and, instead, kept looking at his phone.

"Oh wait, I was gonna pay half, right?"

"Yeah," Staci said, looking at how high the bill was. Their one meal was going to cost her almost four hundred dollars. She knew the place was expensive, but Marcus had decided to order all three courses plus dessert. She wanted him to have a nice time, but at least he was going to pay half the bill.

Marcus patted his pants pockets and then his jacket pockets. He scratched his head.

"What's wrong, baby?"

"I think I left my wallet at home. Wait, let me go check to see if I left it in your car."

She gave him the keys.

The waiter kept circling around to see if the check was ready to be paid.

Marcus walked back in five minutes later, shrugging his shoulders.

"Baby, I really think I left it at home. Do you think I could get you next time? I'm so embarrassed. This has never happened to me before. I always try to make sure I take my wallet. You know I would never do that to you, right?"

"I know, Sweetheart. It's perfectly fine."

Staci took out one of her credit cards and beckoned for the waiter to come by and pick it up.

"But that bill obviously isn't a problem for my baby. We're not all rich." Marcus chuckled.

Staci's facial expression shifted from delight to furrowed eyebrows and a stiff mouth.

"Who said I was rich? I work with the public."

"Baby, don't take it like that. I'm just proud of your success. I'm trying to get like you. Hopefully, the message that I bring to the people on Sunday will get me further to where I want to be."

"It will. God is still in the blessing business."

Marcus leaned back in his chair and said, "Oh, I know he is. I been waiting for my breakthrough for a long time. I think I'm almost there."

Sunday morning service was more upbeat than usual. Staci decided to join the congregation within the first few minutes instead walking in later, as she usually did. The youth praise team had learned a few songs they had heard from more relatable Gospel singers, such as Tye Tribbett.

She felt her heart swoon with joy once she saw all

the children in the front pew standing up and clapping their hands. The choir had grown by more than ten people. A few men had joined. It was always hard to get men to join the choir but their voices held down the baseline so well, the church always got quieter when the choir director pointed at their section to sing alone.

Men in the church were becoming rarer. The only ones left were those that had grown so old, they could barely remember the age they were when they first joined Center of Praise. Women prayed for more men to come to the church and eventually marry them, along with their pew full of children.

Several heads turned around at once, like dominos falling one by one to look at the young man who promised to preach that Sunday. Marcus was dressed in a charcoal gray suit with a gold crucifix chain dangling on top of his black tie. He wore the gold cufflinks Staci had bought for him the last time they went to the mall together. The watch Staci bought him glistened just enough on his wrist. His broad smile appeared once he saw Staci's face.

Staci made a slight wave while clapping and singing along. The usher guided Marcus to the front row of the church, but he declined and walked toward the pulpit. He casually moved past the deacons and sat next to a visiting pastor.

She was surprised that he would be bold enough to come directly to the pulpit, but she admired his confidence. Besides, he was supposed to preach to the one of the largest crowds in Watts, so she knew he should feel comfortable.

Before taking his seat, Staci watched Marcus kneel and pray for a couple minutes. He then began clapping his hands along to the music and nodding toward a few of the deacons. Staci knew they didn't like anyone just hopping into the pulpit, but she knew Marcus meant well. She couldn't wait to hear his message. He had been asking for advice all week on how to improve. Staci told him all she knew, including previews from sermons she planned to deliver later in the month.

His eyes closed while he sang and she watched his mouth move as if he was praying while moving to the music. When the music got faster and one of the saints kicked off a shouting session, Marcus hopped down from the altar and began shuffling his feet. The deacons' faces turned from irritated to jubilant within seconds. Deacon Jameson began "cuttin' a step" himself and ran down the aisle. Staci felt the spirit in the room and began speaking in tongues. At one point, she and Marcus were speaking in tongues together.

Her heart almost melted when she saw tears roll down his eyes after he stopped praying. She loved how he was so grateful for all that God had done for him.

Following the offering, Staci stood up to introduce the speaker.

"Church, I have a special treat for you. I know

you've been waiting and we've all been excited, but the time has finally come! Minister Marcus Vincent is a dynamic preacher from Los Angeles. He's traveled all over, spreading the Gospel of Jesus Christ. This man is saved, sanctified, and you better believe he's filled with the Holy Ghost. Y'all saw him dancing down there! This man is going to bring you nothing but the word. Please help us make Minister Vincent feel at home. Stand up, y'all, and welcome the speaker of the hour!"

The membership stood at the same time and clapped.

Marcus kindly asked them to be seated and then began with his sermon.

"Church, I'd like you to go to Ephesians, chapter six verse eleven. May I have Deacon Jameson read that for me?"

Deacon Jameson stood with his heavy, black Bible

in both hands. He had a hard time squinting in his reading glasses at first.

"Chapter six verse eleven reads, 'put on the whole armor of God that ye may be able to stand against the wiles of the devil.'"

"Thank you, Deacon Jameson. Now, some of you not wearing your whole armor. Some of y'all got it halfway on. Some got it up collecting dust in their closet and others, well, you just didn't buy it at all. I think a whole lot of you think you don't need it! But let me tell you something! You need to put on that whole armor, and I mean every day. You see, the devil don't sleep. He always got that sword in his hand, just waiting to attack his enemy. That devil ready to catch you slippin'!"

The crowd laughed.

"He don't care if you're a mother, father, teacher, or preacher. All he cares about is that you're a child of God and he spiritually caught you with your pants down. Church, tell your neighbor, 'the devil done caught you with your pants down.'"

The crowd repeated the phrase and laughed. He had them hanging on his every word. He made them laugh, think, and even shed a tear.

Staci stood up almost during the entire message. She had her head held high and couldn't stop exchanging pleasant glances with Martha each time he went back to his hook.

She wiped his forehead with a towel and made sure that there was ice cold water available for him while he rested.

Staci stood to make closing remarks.

"Now, church. Wasn't that wonderful? That brother sure can preach, can he? We're going to have prayer and then the benediction."

Staci felt a tug on her jacket.

She brought her ear to his mouth so he could whisper to her.

"Aren't you going to do an offering?" Marcus asked.

"We already did an offering."

"Yeah, but don't you usually do an offering for the speaker? A love offering."

Staci knew that the deacon board would be furious if she went on with it. They specifically said that Center of Praise should never go beyond the "sick and shut-in" offering and the general offering.

Staci went back to the microphone.

"Church? Before we leave here today, I wanted to hold a special offering for our speaker. He really brought the word, and I wanted to be a blessing to him."

The ushers motioned toward her with confused looks on their faces. Staci didn't even want to look at the deacons' facial expressions.

"Everyone can just come up and lay the money down on the altar. Just come at once. We won't need an organized line."

Within minutes, the crowd walked up to the altar and dropped tens, fives, twenties, and even a couple hundreds.

The ushers immediately gathered the money and gave it to the deacon in charge of finances. He counted it right there and handed it to Marcus in two envelopes.

Staci watched Marcus have one of the largest

smiles on his face he had ever seen.

"How much was it?" she asked. Staci directed Deacon Jameson to lead prayer and then the benediction.

"A little under one thousand."

"Wow, that's amazing."

"Is that typical of an offering at church?"

"No. They usually give more than that, of course. However, most love offerings are not that hefty. That's a good chunk of money. You can use that to help you in your prayer app ministry."

Marcus shrugged and put the money away in his coat pocket.

Staci thought he would be more thankful, but he sat there motionless. He only moved his right arm to drink his water.

"Three offerings?" Staci saw Mother Earnestine mouth to Deacon Jameson.

Staci knew she had definitely pissed off a lot of people, but it was only supposed to happen once.

"Maybe next time, I'll get a little more. They're more generous than my last church, though."

"Next time? We usually do it for first time visitors or those we don't see that often."

"So, you're the only preacher getting paid here, huh?" Marcus' shoulders bounced up and down and he shook his head.

"That's not it at all."

The last prayer of the service was said, and two

people decided to officially join the church. Staci walked from the pulpit to give them the right hand of fellowship.

Marcus did, too.

"You don't have to walk down with me," she said, looking back.

"I'm just here for support. They just joined, so they also know me."

Staci felt her stomach drop. If she had been lighter, she knew her whole face would have been red.

Staci finally caught eyes with the board of deacons to the right of her, and their faces said it all. All she could see was two rows of men with their arms crossed over their chests. She could barely make out their faces because the sun behind them had turned most of the men into silhouettes. Staci knew she wasn't going to hear the end of it. She had just gotten on the deacons' good side.

She looked at Marcus, who shook the hands of the new members, and it seemed very natural for him. A thought flashed across her mind that they could possibly be co-pastors one day. He was a natural people person and could hold a conversation with almost anyone he met.

Directly following service, Marcus blended into the crowd and shook the hands of both young and old. Staci wanted to kiss him so badly. He was so handsome when he knelt down to shake the hand of the six-year-old child that was joining the church with his mom.

Staci left Marcus in the auditorium to mingle. She planned on texting him later so they could meet after church.

The deacons followed her into the conference room, where they always started with the counting of the offering money and then went into talking about business matters.

The church offering buckets were delivered to the door and then a few minutes later, there was a loud knock.

They knew better than to open it because many churches in the past had had people brazenly rob them.

"Yes? Who's there?"

"It's me, Minister Vincent."

Several of the deacons shook their heads. No one, except authorized personnel, was allowed into the conference room while they were counting money.

Staci walked over to the door to open it.

"Minister Vincent, we were just getting ready to count up the offering. I'll have to catch up with you later."

"Oh, it's okay. I used to do this with my old pastor all the time. I could probably help you all get it done faster."

"That's okay! We got it," Deacon Jameson said.

"No, it's fine. He's good people."

Staci allowed Marcus to help the deacons count the money. He was so charming that most of them relaxed with him around. He began telling jokes and he had gone to the same Bible college as two of them.

After an hour, Staci decided to wrap up the business meeting. Marcus left early and left the other men to carefully count the rest of the money.

Just as they were about to leave, Deacon Jameson tapped Staci on the shoulder.

"The count was off this time," he whispered.

"We always get about five thousand for the

hospitality offering, we're missing one thousand."

"They probably didn't count it right."

"No, it was counted right after offering in the morning. The usher counted it in front of me and wrote down the amount. This time, the count was off. This never happens."

"Well, it had to be some mistake. Well, all of a sudden, we have someone new counting the money and then it disappears. I'm not trying to point fingers, but it's just strange," he continued.

"Minister Vincent would never. I mean, the man just brought the word. He lives and breathes walking with Jesus."

"I'm just stating the facts, Pastor."

Staci abruptly left the church and allowed two of

the deacons to lock the church doors for the night.

She couldn't wait and called Marcus in the car. She was shaking so much, her finger could barely press the call button.

"Hello?"

"Yes, Marcus. What are you up to right now?"

"Nothing much, Why?"

"The deacons told me that a significant amount of money was missing from our hospitality offering."

"Okay. What does that have to do with me?"

"I just wanted to know if you knew anything."

"Are you accusing me?"

"No, baby. I'm not accusing you of anything. I just wanted to know if you had any information."

"See, I knew this was gonna happen. I bring down the house in your own church and now you're jealous. I thought you were better than that."

"What? Marcus, I was so proud of you. I would never compete with you. I love you."

"Yeah, well you're up here on the phone accusing me of being a thief. I wasn't raised that way. My momma raised me better than that."

"I'm sorry, Marcus. I didn't mean to come off like I was accusing you of something. That wasn't my intention. I was just concerned." Staci's eyes had filled to the brim with tears. She was trying to hold it together.

"Are you crying? I should be the one crying. People up here accusing me of stealing."

"Marcus, look, let's talk about this tonight. I'm sorry, baby."

He breathed a deep sigh. "Alright. I'll talk to you later."

Once she hung up, Staci saw that she had received a text from Martha. Deacon Knight was her great uncle, so she always knew what they were up to.

I heard that somebody stole money. Is that true? Was Minister Vincent counting money?

He was in there, but he was just helping. I didn't want to make it seem like he wasn't welcome.

I thought no one was allowed in the conference room while money is being counted. Staci sent with an angry Emoji.

No. It's fine. We'll figure it out. I'm pretty sure

it was a miscount.

All of a sudden this happened when Marcus visited? Sounds strange.

Just have trust in God that this will all work out.

Staci then sent several texts to Marcus apologizing for what she had said. It was the most begging she had ever done in her life.

It's okay, baby, Marcus texted. **I just want to make sure nothing comes between us. I would never lie to you. I could tell those deacons didn't like me. I don't know who took it but I'm gonna help you in any way I can. You're so special to me, baby.**

I love you, Marcus.

Chapter 6

Brother Lucifer

The candles were lit and placed on her dining room table. The house smelled like cornbread, greens, and the chicken inside her roaster. A pink apron covered her blouse and jean skirt, which fit much tighter than usual. She wore her slippers, but planned on changing into her heels once she got a text that Marcus was closer.

This was the first time she had cooked dinner for anyone other than her parents. She was used to making pasta and simple salads, but she watched hours of YouTube videos on how to cook a nice soul food meal. She even stayed on the phone with her mother when she first started cooking, just to make sure that she was including the right ingredients.

I'm on my way Marcus texted.

Staci began racing around the kitchen, trying to make sure that the dining room table was set up nicely. She had purchased a new table cloth and made a playlist for background music while they were eating.

Staci never had any intention of Marcus coming over to her house. She was afraid that it would lead to the temptation of having sex before marriage. They had a conversation over the phone when she invited him over about her expectations. Her intent was to have a nice dinner for an hour, have some conversation, and then send him on his way. Marcus told her that nothing would go on. He was serious about being celibate, which he claimed to be. He had told her a long time ago that it didn't bother him that she was a virgin.

Her doorbell rang, and Staci's heart could have

jumped out of her chest onto the floor. She removed her apron, put on her heels, and opened it.

Marcus kissed her on the lips immediately while grabbing her waist. He lifted her body up and kissed her once more while she held onto his wide jawline.

"How's my baby been?" he asked.

"I've been fine. I've just been waiting on you. I got a nice dinner in there."

"Look at my girl, doing all this cookin'. I know you love me, don't you?"

"I do, baby." Staci held his hand to lead him into the kitchen. He made a few comments about his favorite foods growing up and then sat at the table.

Removing his jacket, he sat down with his phone in hand. Staci pulled his phone from his fingers and put it face down.

"Baby, now you know this is supposed to be a special time for us. I don't want to get too distracted by our phones. This is a time to relax and reflect."

Marcus turned the alerts off his phone and sat with his arms across his chest until Staci brought out the food.

She presented the cornbread first and then a hot plate of collard greens. The baked macaroni came out next, and then a whole roasted chicken.

"You did some serious cooking, baby."

Staci put both plates, two forks, and two knives on the table near the food. She grabbed his hands and began praying.

"Lord, we come to you today to say thank you for this wonderful meal. Bless the hands that cooked it and the mouths that will partake in it. We just want to say thank you for keeping us and delivering us from a life of sin. Let this meal not harm our bodies. Let it be nutritious to our bodies. In Jesus' name we pray. Amen."

Marcus' left foot was shaking.

"You want to know what's on that phone, huh?" Staci said.

"No. I'm fine. I'm just really hungry."

She continued the conversation about the details of his message from the last time he preached. Marcus' eyes kept landing on her breasts. Part of her cleavage was exposed where part of her blouse was unbuttoned.

Staci buttoned her shirt, and then Marcus quickly looked in the other direction.

"So, how come you've put off marriage so long? I

still can't believe that a gorgeous woman like you was single. It don't make any sense, if you ask me."

"Well, I was in school and trying to become a minister. I just didn't have the time."

"See, I did have the time, but I never met anyone. I joined the app on a whim and then I met you. I really can't believe how much of a blessing that you've been in my life."

Staci took his hand and he squeezed it.

"Let me go get you some dessert for being so sweet," Staci chuckled.

In the kitchen was blueberry pie. Staci knew Marcus loved pie and warmed him up a slice.

"You want some whipped cream on it?" she asked.

"Yes, please!"

"Mind if I check my email?" Marcus asked.

"Yeah, that's fine. How about we move over to the living room?"

Marcus grabbed his phone and headed over to the couch. With his socks on, he put both feet on the couch and laid back. He placed one of her decorative pillows underneath his head.

Staci sat on the love seat opposite of him.

"You think we could share the couch?" she said, staring at his right foot that was on her coffee table. Staci hated feet on her furniture.

"Yeah, baby. Come over here."

Marcus put his feet down and allowed Staci to sit

next to him. He pulled her closer and began kissing her neck and lightly bit her ear.

Staci moved him away at first, but then allowed him to overcome her. His hands were on either side of her body. His pelvis touched hers, and then shivers moved through her body. She had never been this turned on before.

Marcus kissed her softly, starting from her upper neck down to her breasts. He unbuttoned her shirt, but Staci stopped him. She could clearly feel his hard penis pushing against her clothed vagina. Every time she tried to get up, he stopped her with a deep tongue kiss that made her moan.

"Marcus, Marcus. We have to stop. It's too much."

"Stop, what? I love you, baby."

She tried to push his solid arms away, but was

unsuccessful.

Once she saw Marcus unzip his pants and attempt to enter her under her skirt, she shrieked.

"Marcus! We talked about this. No!"

Marcus jumped back with a scowl on his face and stood up.

"So, you just invite me over and think nothin' is going to happen?"

"Yes! I expected nothing to happen. I told you that over the phone. Did you think I was playing?"

"Look, you were coming on to me, too. Don't sit up here and try to act like I was raping you, because I wasn't."

"I never said that, Marcus. I was into it too, but I

had to stop myself. I'm not ready yet."

He had his hands on his forehead and bent over as if he had run out of breath.

"I don't know why you're acting so surprised. I'm a saved woman and I want to wait until I'm married to have sex. I don't think it's that hard."

"Who are you proving this to?"

"God! My Lord and Savior. That's who. You should be as well. I'm a pastor. I'm supposed to be setting an example."

"It seems like every time we talk, you gotta bring up the fact that you're a pastor. Yes, we all know."

"Marcus, I wasn't bringing it up to shame anyone. I just want you to see where I'm coming from."

Marcus had turned his body away from her and had his phone in his hand, pretending to be busy.

"Look, that phone is part of the problem." Staci raged.

"Are you somebody's mama?" Marcus sneered. "Look. I get it. You don't wanna have sex. It's cool. I mean, you act like the whole neighborhood gonna find out."

"Why does it bother you so much?" Staci asked.

She had her hands on both hips, looking at him from across the living room.

"It bothers me because you, literally, invite me over and expect nothing to happen. It's cool, but sex is a very important part of the relationship."

"You're pushing the issue, why? I thought you

were a man of God. You should know where I'm coming from."

"Here you go virtue signaling, like you're the holiest one in the room."

Staci sat on the loveseat across from the couch and refused to look at Marcus any longer. She knew she would break down in tears. Marcus grabbed his coat from the dining room and put his shoes on.

"Yeah, I'm gonna go. I'll see you later."

He walked past her and closed the door behind him.

Staci let the tears flow, like she had been holding them in for years. She had cooked for him, like he wanted, but the moment she didn't give in to having sex, he was furious. He was starting to be a lot less like the man that she first went on a date with.

She put the dishes in the dishwasher and changed out of her clothes to put on pajamas. Staci didn't plan on going anywhere else for the rest of the evening. Part of her wanted Marcus to continue what he was doing, but she knew that it wasn't what she wanted to indulge in yet. If she had been able to remain a virgin for forty years, she could do at least one or two more.

Her anger almost made her want to take him off the preaching schedule, but she didn't want to be petty.

Staci checked her phone and saw that she had missed two texts from Martha. She had told her that she was sending out her Save-the-Dates soon and wanted her to look out for them. Staci forgot all about her closest church confidant getting married. It was noticeable that Martha had been beaming more than usual of late. Her relationship with her fiancé on social media looked perfect. He was always taking her on trips and bought her beautiful jewelry. Martha wore a necklace with her birthstone on it that Staci had complimented before.

She then thought about all the good times she'd had with Marcus. Although he couldn't afford interesting vacations in foreign countries, he did what he could. He was also a humble man who was trying to improve his life by starting his own business.

He hadn't tried to rape her. She figured they both had gotten caught up in the heat of the moment. Staci wanted him as badly as he wanted her. Marcus was more of a touchy-feely person that loved to be hugged and kissed. Staci loved physical touch as well, but it had just gone too far that time.

Thoughts of losing Marcus swam through her head. She was sure that there was no one else out there for her. Other men wouldn't be willing to support her ambitions in the ministry. Most of them wouldn't even be saved.

At forty-years-old and with the possibility of having children getting slimmer every day, she wanted to hold onto the man that showed her at least some affection. Besides a few hiccups, Staci was confident that their relationship could work. Couples counseling before marriage and opportunities to work on their communication were all she felt they needed.

She texted him to see if he would respond.

Hello, Marcus. I'm sorry about what happened. Can you talk?

He didn't respond that day and the next.

Every moment of the day had Staci on edge. Into the week, while she sat in meetings and met with her publisher about her second book, she was constantly jumping whenever her phone made a sound.

He was still active on social media because she saw him post a picture with him and his cousins.

She texted him again while on her way to her car after a business meeting at church.

Marcus, what's going on? Can we talk about this?

Talk about what? He responded quickly.

Talk about what happened last time we saw each other. I don't want to be like this.

I can't talk right now. I'm with my business partners but I'll talk as soon as I can.

His response was reassuring to her. He didn't seem as angry as before.

❖

One week later, Staci looked for Marcus to walk into the church.

He never did.

She looked for him the following Sunday.

He was a no-show once again.

Staci had become so distracted by what was going on with Marcus that she was starting to become more absent-minded during important meetings. The deacons and Martha could tell that something was up.

"What's going on, Staci?" Martha whispered, walking two steps behind Staci as she walked toward her car.

"Nothing. I'm fine."

"You don't seem like yourself. Is it about that man? I notice he hasn't been to church in the last two weeks. Is everything okay?"

"We had a minor argument two weeks ago," Staci sighed. "It's not that important."

"Well, what happened? You haven't been yourself. You usually talk the most during meetings."

"I'm just waiting on him to propose and I'm getting a little impatient. That's all."

"Propose?" Martha said while Staci slid into the driver's seat of her car.

"Yeah. It's nothing really. I'm just ready to start a family and I'm not getting any younger."

"Have you prayed about it?"

"I have. I know this is the one God sent for me. He has all the qualities I've ever wanted and needed in a husband."

"Well, I would just say to trust God. Are you sure God said him?"

"Why would you say that?"

"He just doesn't strike me as the most husband material type of guy. I mean, he's never been married. I don't think he's that genuine. That's just me. He reminds me of my uncles that either cheated or wanted girlfriends their whole lives."

"Now, Marcus is not that at all. He's a saved man and he does right by God. He wants a family. He loves me. He wants to support me."

"He doesn't see you as a threat? Not too many men can handle a woman in leadership."

"Oh no. Marcus loves what I do. Besides, it inspires him to move further with his prayer app and moving up in the ministry."

"How long has he been working on this app? Have you met the people he works with?"

"I trust God. Marcus has no reason to lie to me. You should learn to be happy for others, Martha. You're not the only one cut out for marriage. Other people would like to be happy, too."

Martha shrugged her shoulders and stepped away from Staci's car.

Staci slammed her door and drove off into the darkening street toward home.

❖

"Are you on your way?" Staci asked.

"Yeah. I'm almost there."

She called Marcus while nervously putting on her makeup and then attempting to roll her stockings up to her waist.

Her hair had been pressed straight with a deep part. A sparkly barrette matched her purse that she had just ordered from the internet. Staci sprayed some of her best perfume on and then sat on her bed.

She and Marcus had been arguing more than usual lately, but had cleared up most of their differences so they could attend Martha's wedding on Saturday.

Marcus met her at the door and held her hand to lead her into the passenger's seat. He drove and turned the heat on since it was slightly chilly outside.

Martha's wedding was going to be held indoors at a hotel, so they wouldn't be exposed to the elements for too long.

"You know, I really missed you when we weren't talking," Marcus confessed.

"I missed you too, and that was hard. I don't want to do that again."

"It won't happen again."

They continued light conversation for the rest of the forty-five minutes it took to get to the hotel in Malibu. Staci noticed that Marcus didn't check his phone once. This was one of the first opportunities she'd had in a long time to just talk to him without distractions.

Once they arrived at the hotel, Marcus took her hand to guide her out of the car. She loved how gentle he was with her. Every time she looked into his eyes, she felt like she was in another, more perfect world.

She didn't even notice when they walked into the room where the ceremony was being held. It was like they had glided inside.

Martha walked out thirty minutes later. Her heart swelled when she saw her fiancé cry. It was her biggest dream to have a man cry over her when she walked down the aisle, toward the altar.

Martha was beautiful. Her veil trailed behind her on the floor, held up by a four-year-old flower girl. Her dress was fitted and curved around her waist mermaid-style. It seemed like her makeup was so flawless, like it was painted on. The earrings in her ears dazzled while they reflected against the chandeliers.

"Don't they look beautiful?" Staci whispered.

Marcus nodded his head and took out his phone.

Staci shook her head. She was tired of chastising him about his phone, so she decided to keep her comments to herself.

Directly following the wedding, the crowd went to the large dining hall with tables and chairs set up with white and silver everywhere.

"No open bar?" Marcus said in Staci's ear.

"Um, no. This is a Christian wedding. They're not even dancing. She was going to have praise dancers instead."

Marcus rolled his eyes.

Staci helped lead him to his seat once they found their names on the chart.

Following their entrance and then prayer, Martha found Staci in the crowd and hugged her.

"You look so beautiful! This is such a beautiful place to have a wedding."

Martha thanked her and said that if she had any concerns or suggestions, she could talk to her wedding planner and coordinator directly. Staci sat at the head table with the bridal party and other honorees.

Staci said the prayer over the food, and then the room buzzed with compliments for the bride and groom.

While everyone was intermingling, Marcus decided to play a word game on his phone.

"Look, let's get up and say 'hello' to Deacon Brown and Deacon Jameson."

"Why? Those the ones that accused me of stealing. I don't wanna talk to them."

Staci thought he sounded like an insolent child, but ignored him and continued to mingle with everyone else in the dining room.

Staci and Marcus returned to their car around 10:30 PM.

Marcus didn't open the passenger's side door to let Staci in, as he usually did.

"Is everything okay?" Staci said, getting into the car. "You seem a little irritated. Are you tired?"

"I'm okay. I just. I don't know."

"No. Tell me, baby," Staci said while placing her hand on his thigh.

"It's just that Martha and her new husband are so young, and it made me realize how much of my life is not together. It kind of makes me feel like less of a man."

"You shouldn't feel that way, baby. I don't think of you as less of a man for any reason. We'll go down that road soon enough."

"Yeah. We will. I mean, the ceremony was nice but I plan on doing so much better than that one day. I already looked at venues. I saw a place in Rancho Palos Verdes. It was by the water. I want to do it big for my woman."

"Okay, then that's what we'll do, my love. Martha had always been so ambitious, though. Everyone says she's been ready to get married since she was a teenager. I don't think I was thinking about marriage at that age. I'm sure you weren't either."

"Well, I was too busy looking for the perfect woman. See, that's why so many people get divorced. They're not looking for that right person. They're just trying to get married."

"I agree," Staci said, nodding her head. "Some folk just want a party. I mean. We're halfway there. You gave me a promise ring. You also said you'd promise to be there this Sunday. That would be more special than anything you could ever do for me. I just want to see you in church."

"You're right. I need to be back in the house of the Lord. Do you think I could bring the word this Sunday?"

It was as if the only time Marcus wanted to come to church was when he could be in front of the people bringing the message.

"That's fine. I'll make sure you're on the calendar. We just hired a full-time secretary, Ashley. I'll tell her. Martha doesn't do it anymore."

"You got somebody else on payroll?" Marcus asked with one eyebrow raised.

"I mean. Just one more person."

"Well, I'll say," Marcus said under his breath.

He turned music on for the rest of the ride.

Staci closed her eyes and sank into her seat. She

twisted the ring around her finger until her body relaxed and the car ride rocked her to sleep.

❖

Two weeks later, Staci got a text from Marcus. It was Saturday night and she had finally gotten some time to herself. She had cancelled her meeting with the youth department and scheduled to wrap herself up in blankets with one of her favorite romantic comedies.

Baby, put on your best dress. We going out tonight.

What? Where? She texted back quickly.

I'll pick you up in an hour. It's a surprise.

Staci hopped out of her blankets in seconds and rushed to her closet to find one of her evening gowns. She pulled out a gold, sparkly one that flowed down to her ankles. It had one shoulder and revealed more of her cleavage than she wanted to, but Marcus rarely took her out by surprise. She had worn it to her cousin's wedding in Alabama two years ago and it still fit.

She tossed her hair up with a few curls hanging down. A gold clip gripped the side of her updo for extra flair.

Marcus arrived at her house in exactly an hour. He had roses in his hand when he met her at the door.

"Marcus, what's all this?"

"Just something a little special for my girl."

The ride over to the restaurant was filled with laughs and more conversation than Staci had gotten out of Marcus in a long time.

She loved the way he gripped her thigh at the

stoplight and sneaked a quick kiss on her cheek when she wasn't looking.

Once they arrived at the restaurant, Staci felt like a celebrity. Their table was ready once they walked in, and the lit candle in the middle of the table was a beautiful touch.

After they ate, Marcus gently gripped Staci's hand.

"Baby, there's been something I've been wanting to do for a long time."

Staci covered her mouth when she gasped and the hand within his began shaking.

Marcus got down on one knee and took out a black box. Tears began to well up in Staci's eyes.

"You know I've been wanting to make it official with you for a long time. I don't want to wait any longer. I truly believe that God sent you to be the one for me."

The two had been dating for a little under six months, but had already gone through about as much as some couples experience in two years.

The tears on Staci's face ended up on her chest.

The restaurant had sparse attendance, so they weren't getting much attention from the other patrons.

"Would you marry me, Staci?"

"Yes! Yes, Marcus! I will!"

The ring had a silver band with a small diamond surrounded by rubies in the shape of a heart.

It wasn't the ring that Staci expected, but it was the one she knew she was going to love.

After the proposal, they kissed and then sat across from each other. The couple couldn't stop staring into each other's eyes. Staci then focused her attention on her ring.

"This is beautiful, Baby."

She took a sip of water and continued.

"What date are we thinking? I can't even think straight right now. I'm just shocked."

"Well, how about exactly one year from now?" Marcus cooed in his velvety baritone that still made Staci swoon.

"I was actually thinking sooner. More like six months or a little less?"

"I don't mind. That's going to be a short time to plan our big wedding."

"Well, I was thinking of something small. I'm more comfortable with that. Actually, we could just do one on a Sunday and include all the members plus our family. That'll be bigger, but it won't take as much planning."

"Yeah. Whatever you want, Baby."

Staci allowed Marcus to clutch her arm so they could walk toward the balcony and overlook the beach. The ocean waves crashed against jagged rocks, and only a few people were left on the beach strolling with their partner.

"I can't wait to tell the church on Sunday," Staci whispered as Marcus held her around the waist. "That's okay with you, right?"

"It's fine with me. I think the church should be in on our happiness."

Staci began texting everyone who was closest to

221

her, including Martha. She asked her not to tell the church yet. She wanted to tell them on Sunday.

Her mother called her within minutes of receiving the text. She could tell her mother was so excited that she might faint.

Staci's world was lining up just as she'd planned. She was getting married to a handsome minister in her own church within months. Besides having a baby, she couldn't ask God for anything more. He had answered her prayers and sent her the man she had needed to have by her side.

God was good. All the time.

❖

Staci gripped the pulpit and scanned the crowd. Over seventy members had joined since she took over the ministry.

No one had ever seen a larger youth choir and the praise dance team had grown so much, young men had started a miming ministry team.

She had hired a new choir director from Atlanta that turned the choir into one of the best in California. They had been recorded singing background for Fred Hammond on his latest album. The deacons were happy that more money was coming in than being spent.

The church had even begun to do more outreaches for the community, which made Staci's heart swell with pride every time they gave away school supplies and shoes for elementary school students.

Staci hadn't spoken yet, but a calm fell across the auditorium while she smiled at her members. She loved all of them. They were like family.

"Church, I know many of you remember when I first came here. I wasn't as talkative. I doubted myself and

I was on my knees two to three times a day, begging God to lead me in the right path. Although I talk to so many of you, many of you may not know that I had been asking God for a husband."

The people collectively gasped.

"Minister Vincent and I are getting married."

Rows of people stood up at once and loudly congratulated their pastor.

"I want all of you," Staci continued, "to be part of the ceremony. It will be held here very soon. I promise, I won't keep you all waiting. Minister Vincent and I are very happy to work together in this church."

Staci saw Marcus had stood from his seat. She could feel his eyes locked in on her.

"Co-pastors?" Someone shouted from the crowd.

"No. Not at this time. I think one pastor is enough," she laughed.

Staci quickly looked back at Marcus and saw him try to hide the anger in his face. He looked away and sat down. He opened his Bible and started pretending to read it.

She hoped she hadn't hurt his feelings, but he had never expressed wanting to be a co-pastor before. Besides, Marcus had only recently received his elder's license three weeks ago. Staci had pushed him to keep going and she had a celebratory dinner in his honor at the church a few days after it was finalized.

Staci took her seat and tried to get eye contact with Marcus, but it was obvious he was trying to focus on everything but her.

There was a possibility he was offended that she had called him a minister instead of an elder. He would have almost as much authority as she would and he had been privy to the way the church ran for months. Marcus had only been coming to the church regularly for the last month. He was off and on when it came to attending weekly meetings, so she assumed he wasn't serious about assuming leadership one day.

Staci sat closer to his side of the pulpit and tapped him on the shoulder. He didn't respond at first, but then looked up to meet her gaze.

"Everything okay, Elder?" Staci whispered.

"No. I'm fine," Marcus said, talking behind a church program to hide their moving lips from the crowd.

"It was okay that I announced that it would be at the church, right?"

"No. I have no problem with that. You did what you had to do," he said snappily.

His statement gave Staci an odd feeling in the pit of her stomach.

"I'll sort it all out. Don't you worry," he said, patting her on the shoulder.

Confused, Staci sat in her center pulpit chair and continued on with the service.

Marcus was as stoic as a statue for the rest of service before he disappeared just before benediction. He gave no handshakes or nods to anyone he passed by before he left.

No one, except Staci, noticed. Yet, this time, her heart felt heavier than it ever had since she met him.

All she could do was pray.

Chapter 7

Blindsided

Staci was elated that Marcus was coming to church more than usual lately. He was at every meeting, right by her side. He preached almost every other Sunday and even led Sunday school. He was beginning to become as visible as she was.

Following service on a bright Sunday in the middle of April, Staci said the benediction as always.

The church stood and said the closing prayer in unison, and then the last song.

God be with you!
God be with you!

God be with you, until we meet again!

The membership dispersed into all directions, and the ushers erected a velvet rope and a stool so Staci could sit and greet a few of the people that stayed behind.

Marcus stayed nearby and stood his post a few feet away from Staci. He also shook hands with the people and quickly prayed for those that requested it.

While shaking hands with one of the visitors, Staci noticed that Marcus was speaking to one of the new members, a woman of about thirty that had a ten-year-old son. He kept the conversation going with her than anyone else that had come by. Staci was still shaking hands with anyone that came by, but she kept her right ear on their conversation like a satellite because he wasn't whispering.

"How do you feel about someone like me becoming a pastor one day, if there were ever to become an opening?" Marcus said to the woman. He tried to keep his voice low, but Staci heard him loud and clear.

"I mean, I really like you're preaching. It wouldn't bother me. Is Pastor Bernard planning on leaving?"

"No. I was just asking. I wanted to get your opinion. I mean, not necessarily this church, but the pastor of a church this size is something I might want to explore."

They began to talk some more but Staci had gotten distracted by Todd, who almost ran up to her.

"Pastor, can we have you sit in our music department meeting? We would truly appreciate your wisdom right now."

"I'll be there in a second, Todd. Thank you!"

She nodded at the ushers to begin putting the velvet rope away. They removed her chair, and the stragglers in the crowd began to file out of the auditorium.

Staci saw Marcus leaving the building out of the corner of her eye and asked to speak to him.

He was quickly walking to his car and paused when he heard the quick steps from Staci's heels.

"I thought I was going to see you a little later, baby?" Marcus asked.

Staci lowered her voice. "I heard you talking to that young woman."

"And? Don't tell me you about to get jealous."

Marcus pressed his keychain to open his car. He put one foot inside, but Staci moved closer.

"Nobody is getting jealous. I just heard something you said that was kind of strange. You asked her how she would feel about you being pastor."

Marcus shook his head and laughed. His body tilted backward.

"You heard me wrong. I don't remember saying that. Besides, it was loud in there."

"I know what I heard Marcus. It's fine. I do want to support your ambitions of being a pastor."

"I'll talk to you later, Staci."

Marcus lowered his head to get into his car and backed out of the parking spot in a rush. He left Staci there with arms crossed, shaking her head. She was already late for the Music Department meeting, so she decided to take her time to get to the music office.

Marcus had been much more involved in the church and was still singing and shouting, like he always had. However, there was something off about him that she couldn't quite put her finger on.

Staci finally made it inside the Music Department meeting but noticed that Deacon Jameson and Deacon Johnson were talking in the kitchen. One of them mentioned her name, so she became quiet and stopped walking. She took her heels off so she wouldn't make any noise as she got closer to them.

Staci heard Deacon Jameson's voice loud and clear. He was sipping a cup of coffee with his feet on the dining table in front of him.

"Well, I don't know who to believe," he began. "But Elder Vincent told us that he writes all Pastor Bernard's sermons. He also said that she steals some of her ideas from preachers online."

"Now, that's not right," Deacon Jameson sneered.

"It's not, but I knew she was too good. I never heard a woman preach like that before."

Staci wanted to storm in there and set them both straight. Marcus had never written anything for her, and she never plagiarized anyone's sermons. However, Marcus had done it twice, but she didn't say anything because she knew he was just starting out. She couldn't believe that he had been talking to her most trusted deacons behind her back. Deacon Jameson and Deacon Johnson had been the most difficult to win over because they had been at the church the longest.

"I heard that Bishop T.D. Jakes was supposed to come through but because he wasn't offering the church any money, she asked him not to come."

"Just selfish," Deacon Johnson scoffed. "I knew she wasn't no good. See, I was the main one trying to give her a chance. I actually thought she'd be a good fit at one point. Both her and Todd get on my nerves now."

"Well, get this," Deacon Jameson continued. "Elder Vincent warned that we should be careful of her trying to get rid of the whole deacon board."

"She can do that?" Deacon Johnson almost shrieked.

"Well, I wouldn't put anything past her. I mean, she likes to do stuff over our heads all the time. She done spent all this money on the youth. She's always catering to those kids."

The tears began to stream down Staci's face faster than bullets. She knew being a pastor was going to be hard, but nothing could have prepared her for it being this hard. If Marcus had told the deacons these lies, there was no telling what other damage he had done.

She texted Todd that she wasn't feeling well and wouldn't be able to make it to the meeting. She started her car and could barely put it in drive because her hands were still shaking.

Staci picked up her phone and texted Martha.

Martha, has Marcus been telling you anything about me? Be honest.

No. He hasn't. Martha responded in seconds. **Why? Something happened?**

I just overheard the deacons talking crazy. You know how Deacon Jameson is.

Yeah, I know. He can be a trip. He's so evil, though. It doesn't mean he got it from Marcus.

That's true.

But I've been meaning to ask you. How's the wedding planning going?

It's fine, but Marcus has a few ideas of his own. We're fine, though. We're doing well. How are you and

the hubby?

Just fine, Pastor!

Staci put her phone down and then put the car in drive. Her short conversation with Martha had calmed her down.

She wanted to call Marcus and get some answers, but she knew that would only lead to fighting. Marcus had absolutely shared that she didn't write her own sermons. Staci was the most offended by that. Sermon writing had been her specialty in college. Now that she had her doctorate, she had gotten so good at it, other ministers had asked her to write for them. Marcus would ask her to write for him, or at least make suggestions.

At home, she removed her clothing and didn't even pull her nightgown on before she collapsed into the bed.

She called Marcus twice, but he didn't answer. She

left a message. Marcus called back an hour later. Staci was almost in a deep sleep when she heard her cellphone ring.

"Marcus!" she yelled. "What have you been doing? Why can't you answer your phone?"

"Is that the way you answer the phone? I don't know what your momma taught you."

Staci wanted to begin the conversation with what she heard from Deacon Jameson so badly, but she held her tongue. It was too late to argue before bed. She hated going to bed crying into her pillow. Unfortunately, it seemed like as the wedding got closer, she was doing that far more often.

"Marcus, I just want to talk. Every relationship needs communication and we don't live together. We need it."

"Okay, what do you want to talk about," Marcus

said, chewing on chips in her ear, which irritated her. Staci hated when people ate in your ear on the phone.

"Well, I would like to start making some key moves to get this wedding going."

"I've been meaning to talk about that. I think we should do something grander. I don't want to use that church. I have people I know all over the place, and I don't want them venturing into Watts. It's dangerous."

"Oh, so all of a sudden, Watts is dangerous. We're there more than several times a week. Come on, Marcus!"

"Again, this is all about you and not what we both want!"

"Give me your ideas, Marcus," Staci sighed.

"I'll email them to you. I have an alternate venue. I'm looking at three hundred people or more. I'm actually not interested in having the church members there because I don't know them."

"But, Marcus. I promised all of them that they would be invited."

"Well, they're just going to have to be uninvited because I have more important people in my life that actually matter."

"The church is my family. I'm not going to let them down."

"Okay. Are you marrying them or me? Please tell me!"

Staci's head began to hurt; she felt pain in her lower back. Her relationship and the church were beginning to take a toll on her body.

"Marcus, I'm marrying you. I don't want to argue.

We just cannot argue like this before the wedding. We just cannot. I truly care about you and I don't want to go down this road. If we don't look like a unit, the church will see."

"Unit? You don't want a unit. You want to do this all by yourself."

"Marcus, you *just* got your elder's license. You are an official elder in the church. You preach just as much as I do. We aren't married yet. You have no idea what I planned on doing once we got married."

"You women are all the same. You make me feel good in the beginning but when it gets down to the wire, your career is more important than your family. My ex was like you. It was all her credentials and job over me."

"Why are you comparing me to her? Marcus, I want to be partners with you. I want to be your wife. I want you to have a bigger role in the church."

"No, you don't. You had that whole deacon board and then someone chose you. It's all about who you know these days."

"No, it isn't. I worked hard for my position. I thought we talked about this, Marcus."

Staci was sweating so much, she went into the bathroom to put on more deodorant.

"Marcus, if I wasn't in a relationship with you, I'd say you were a little jealous. I really don't know why."

"Jealous? Of you? You must be crazy."

"*You* want to be the pastor. I think you're trying to turn people against me."

"You think whatever you want in your crazy head. Actually, this wedding is off. I don't need to be with a woman that wants to compete."

"Marcus! What are you saying? You can't do this!"

"I can do whatever I want, woman!"

Staci cried the loudest she ever had in her life. There weren't enough tears in her eyes after a few minutes.

Marcus listened to her cry for a few minutes. "For the Bible says, the day of the Lord Is coming. Cruel with fury and burning anger."

"What are you trying to say?" Staci said, catching her breath.

"Oh, you'll find out soon enough."

Marcus hung up the phone and left Staci drowning in her own tears that soaked in her pillow. She could barely breathe and began coughing.

He had been the one person she could confide in.

Everyone else felt more like an acquaintance. He knew her deepest secrets. He knew some things even her own parents didn't know.

Her heart began palpitating as she thought about the potential secrets he would spill to everyone she knew. It was time for an emergency meeting with her deacons. She texted her secretary to put a meeting with her deacons on the calendar. It was going to be an hour and would be held directly after church on Sunday.

Her secretary texted her back.

Pastor, I actually just received a text from Elder Vincent who also wanted to meet with the board directly after church. Was I supposed to put that in the calendar?

He did what? What is the meeting about?

He didn't specify.

It's cancelled. He is no longer allowed to suggest meetings for the board.

Yes, Pastor.

Please alert them that this is an emergency business meeting.

Yes, Pastor.

Staci knew that Marcus had to have a few tricks up his sleeve but if God was on her side, he wouldn't prevail.

Staci began with social media and sent a status talking about how her sermons are always original for those that have been asking. She wrote about how she focused on sermon writing the most in theology school and was open to anyone wanting to ask her for tips and advice. She also wanted to remind the members to be kind to everyone and to keep her in their prayers.

She received over one hundred comments in support of her. One of the members that heard the plagiarism rumor sent a comment that said that she had never heard anyone preach like her before and could always tell it was original.

Staci thanked that commenter and recognized that it was the woman that Marcus had spoken to about him taking over the church.

She turned on relaxing music and promised to start writing down ideas tomorrow. She had a lot to say to the deacon board, but she didn't want to overwhelm them. It would be a short, but concise meeting.

It was time to drive the devil out of the church.

❖

Sunday had come, and Staci was itching to finally have her meeting with the deacons. All of them seemed either irritated or smug in their section. Marcus gave her very little eye contact. Staci gave the message and preached about loving those who may not love you back.

"Church, it's so easy to love those who love you. That's the easy part. However, it's so hard to love those who may not love you. You got to love those that hate you. You got to love those that talk behind your back. You got to love those that are waiting to backstab you. You got to love your enemy. We got to be more like Jesus. It wasn't easy for him to have everlasting love for some, but he did it. Church, there's only one person you are allowed to hate," she paused, "and that's the devil. Your fellow man, you can't hate him. You can hate that spirit, but you can't hate him."

She had all ears and eyes on her. A few stood up in support. One woman, holding her infant, had tears in her eyes. She led the church into a united praise. Todd jumped on the organ and began playing upbeat music so the members could shout. Even the deacons' frowns disappeared. Deacon Jameson left his post and began dancing while speaking in tongues. Staci had felt the spirit so much, it almost knocked the breath out of her and she had to sit down. In her peripheral vision, she caught Marcus on his knees with a single tear streaming down his face.

Staci went over to him and began praying along with her fiancé. She asked God to bless him and continue to protect him.

"Lord, if it is in your will. Bless him in leadership one day," Staci whispered.

The service ended on a high note. Staci made a signal to Deacon Jameson that she was headed to the back of the church to start the meeting.

Staci arrived at the conference room five minutes ahead of schedule, but no one was there. Deacon Johnson was usually the first one in his seat ready to lay out his grievances.

Martha walked by holding her little nephew's hand on her way to put his choir robe back.

"Pastor Bernard, all the deacons are in the church library. They must have gotten confused."

"I never said that anyone was supposed to meet in the library."

Staci rushed past Martha, almost knocking her five-year-old nephew down. She didn't know heels could take her through a hallway so quickly, but she raced like she had on sneakers.

When she opened the door to the library, all eyes were on her.

Marcus was standing in between them with his hands in his pockets. His eyes were so squinted while focusing on her, she could barely see them. All the other deacons looked the same. Shadows of eyes all perched on her. Deacon Jameson had his back turned while shaking his head.

"So, you thought you were going to get away with it?" Marcus began.

"You were not authorized to lead a meeting today. Everyone, our meeting was scheduled in the conference room. I need everyone in there," she commanded.

No one moved. Deacon Johnson bit into a powdered donut and scoffed. "Get away with what?"

"We've noticed that money in the accounts has gone missing," Deacon Johnson began. "The hospitality account has been reduced to almost zero."

"I've been watching the accounts. I just went to the bank," Staci said, frowning.

"To take money out," Deacon Brown smirked.

"No, I didn't! I would never! Marcus, I trusted you to take the money to the bank for us. It was sealed."

"Are you accusing me?" Marcus asked, almost squealing. "Not you with that Louis bag you wear and Louboutin shoes."

"Those were gifts from my parents for my birthday! I paid half for my shoes! I didn't use the church's funds! I never do! I've been able to use the royalties from my books."

"Well, something is wrong and we're gonna find out today," Deacon Jameson groaned.

"So, you're up here changing the traditions of the church *and* stealing? Staci, how could you? Your church trusted you," Marcus taunted.

"Marcus, I have put nothing but blood, sweat, and tears into this church! I have given my life to every program we run here. I do nothing without the approval of all of you, and this is how you all act?"

Staci was trying to keep the tears back with all her strength. She felt more afraid than sad.

"This spending into the youth department has been draining the church!" Deacon Johnson shouted. "The church was just fine before. Deacon Mattison is probably spinning in his grave!"

"You said yourself that the youth department was one of the best things this church has seen in years!"

"Until you started making it the main event!" he shouted back.

Staci caught Marcus shed a half smile. He took two steps closer to Staci.

"Sweetheart, look at the facts. I have a dozen men with me. All of us are lying?"

"Yes! All of you are lying. You've told them nothing but lies!"

Staci took a step backward. Her heart could almost jump out of her chest. Marcus looked so sinister that he was almost unrecognizable to her.

"I can explain. I'll explain everything and figure it out. This is all just some big misunderstanding. This is a church. We got to let God lead."

Marcus looked behind himself, placed his foot on a chair, and focused on Staci like he was trying to win a staring contest. He then took out his phone and read from it.

"First Timothy, second chapter, verses eleven through fifteen. It says, 'a woman should learn in quietness and full submission. I do not permit a woman to teach or have authority over a man. She must be silent.'"

"That's an antiquated belief. The Church of God in Christ just stopped taking that scripture literally," Staci retorted.

"Literally? I take everything in the Bible literally. Are you, Pastor, trying to say that the Bible is wrong? How dare you?"

"I wasn't saying that, Elder Vincent."

Marcus continued. "Well, gentlemen, technically we aren't following the Bible. Now you know, as a man of God, I don't like not following the Bible."

"Yes, sir. Gotta stay with the Bible," Deacon Brown croaked.

"Technically, we're sinning by even having you in

the pulpit as our pastor."

"I was chosen by the Bishop."

"The Bishop is trying to go with all this new age stuff. He's not listening to what the people want. Then again, it isn't even all about you being a woman. You haven't been doing right by the church."

"You know nothing of what you're talking about. I will not be crucified in my own church. You have no facts!"

"Crucified? Oh Lord, men, she think she's Jesus!"

Everyone, besides Staci, laughed heartily.

She began to feel a sharp migraine and had to take a seat.

The rest of the men in the room grilled her about

the money missing in other accounts. Staci had never touched money outside the church. She knew it had to be Marcus that had stolen it. However, he had somehow successfully convinced the deacons to turn against her.

For an hour, she went back and forth with everyone. Marcus had filled their heads with so much false information, it was overwhelming.

Just as Staci saw that most people were getting tired and wanted to go home, she was heartbroken when Marcus decided to reveal one more item that would be the straw that broke the camel's back.

He pulled a tablet out of his briefcase and typed in his password to one of his social media accounts.

"For those of you who think I'm lying, you can look here."

On his tablet was a fake social media page filled

with pictures of her and shots of vacation pictures from the internet. Staci had never gone anywhere further than Hawaii and Jamaica but, apparently, she had pictures of herself on exotic vacations. There weren't any close-ups of her, but he had included enough of her selfies that it looked like the page belonged to her.

To a keen eye, the social media page looked like it had been thrown together but to seventy and eighty-year-old men who could barely send a text, it was the smoking gun.

"Marcus, now you know that isn't me!"

He had even created a username for her as PastorStaci2k19.

"Deacons, I'm serious. I would not put on such a display of extravagance, especially at the cost of the church. It just doesn't make sense."

"Well, I see it right in front of me!" Deacon Jameson chuckled. "I mean, it just can't get no worse. This woman played us all like fools."

"Woman? I am your pastor, Deacon Jameson. You could at least respect me that much."

"Well, maybe we don't want you as pastor anymore. You know, unlike most COGIC churches, we have one of the strongest deacon boards in this city," Deacon Bridges seethed. "That mean, according to our Church's charter of 1975, during Bishop Mattison's tenure, we are allowed to vote a pastor out. The only reason you were voted in is because we had no one else. Apparently, that's not the case anymore."

Staci's heart dropped. Her muscles stiffened and the blood in her veins felt like it had stopped flowing for a second. She felt dryness in her mouth, and there were no tears available to cry.

"What are you trying to say, Deacon?"

"I'm trying to say that I think it's time we have a vote. Don't worry. Majority rules. I'm not a mind reader."

Marcus kept his head down with his arms crossed over his chest.

"Then, you all can do what you have to do. I know I'm innocent."

"You can't appeal it, Pastor. Once we vote and sign, it's done."

"That's fine. It doesn't mean I'll never pastor again."

Staci had fallen in love with Center of Praise for one year and a half. She had done more for that church than she could have ever imagined. She had made history as the first female pastor of the Church of God in Christ. There would be no greater hurt than watching the disappointment on her parents' faces when she told them. Her mother would also have to be further pained by the dissolution of her engagement.

"Marcus," Staci twisted her engagement ring off her finger. "You can have your jewelry back. I don't think it symbolizes what it was meant to anymore."

Marcus quietly took the ring from her hands and put it in his pocket.

The room was silent, except for the loud chewing from Deacon Johnson on yet another powdered donut. He was a heavyset man, so his chair kept creaking. For a moment, Staci couldn't tell if she was hearing the squeak the deacon made with his chair or sounds of her body shutting down as a warning she might faint.

"I'll start," Deacon Jameson began. "I would like all those in favor of Pastor Bernard remaining as our shepherd from here on out, please raise your hand silently."

No one raised their hand. Marcus' shoulders moved as if he was trying to hide his laughter. Deacon Jameson waited thirty seconds for a response.

"Alright," he sighed. "All those in favor of Pastor Bernard discontinuing her leadership of Center of Praise as our shepherd, please raise your hands."

Everyone raised their hand, including Marcus.

"Then it is done. Someone, call the secretary in here to write up our declaration. We will all sign it. Every deacon must write their full name as well as the year you first joined Center of Praise."

"Well, now who's the pastor? We'll have to vote all over again," Deacon Johnson snapped.

Deacon Jameson looked around. "All those in favor of inviting Elder Vincent as our interim pastor until he is installed by the Bishop, raise your hand."

Everyone raised their hand.

Staci lowered her head and only lifted it to focus on the deacons that had been praying for her downfall since she took the position.

They had a charter, and there was nothing she could do but back out of the doorway and try to pretend that it was all a bad dream and none of it happened.

"Congratulations, Elder," Staci said while pushing the doors of the library open so she could exit.

Her tears couldn't come fast enough. She could barely see by the time she got to her car.

Martha had been lingering around with her husband and a few choir members, so she noticed Staci run toward her car.

"Pastor? Pastor! Did they move the meeting? I

heard everyone got it wrong and went to the wrong place. Those old fogeys."

Staci stared at her while clutching the door to her car. Her makeup had streamed down her face. She was almost unrecognizable.

"Pastor?"

"I'm not your pastor anymore, Martha. I have to go."

Staci pulled herself into her car and had trouble driving away because the tears were still making it hard to see.

On the way home, she had to pull over and cry. The one man that had promised to love her had destroyed her livelihood. Part of her blamed herself because she felt she had been too trusting. Thoughts kept spinning around in her head about all the people that had potentially done her wrong. It was possible that no one had been on her side and the whole scheme was to replace her with a male.

The Bible had clearly said that a woman was not supposed to lead men and, from her failure at holding on to the church, she knew she had proven everyone right.

From now on, she would be known as the first woman to pastor a church and be ousted. Her name would be the subject of rumors for years.

No one would know the truth about Marcus and how his whole plan was to become pastor himself. She could never run the church without the approval of the deacons, and he was smart enough to turn them against her. It was only a matter of time before the entire church would turn their back on her and deny that they had ever been pastored by a woman. Marcus had turned her into a scandal for years to come.

Martha texted her.

Staci, you're still my pastor. I don't care what anyone says. That man is a liar! I told you he was a liar! You didn't believe me! I don't believe you stole anything and that page someone linked you to was obviously fake! I can't believe this!

Martha, it's okay. Sometimes God works in ways we don't understand. Keep me in your prayers and hopefully, someday, God will heal my broken heart.

From that Marcus?

No, Martha. My true love. The church.

Chapter 8

Well Connected and

Disrespected

Staci had cried so much that following week, she had to buy eye drops to keep her eyes moist. Even looking at her closet with all the fancy suits she had collected through the years brought a sinking feeling to her stomach. She had never been fired from anything before, but being fired from God's house had to be one of the worst feelings in the world. The only pastors she had known that had been forced to step down had either had extramarital affairs or embezzled funds from the church. Staci had done none of those, but there was no impartial jury that would ever hear her side of the story.

Marcus hadn't texted or called her since that fateful meeting in the library. She didn't want to talk to him, but part of her wanted an explanation about why he did what he did. Her heart wanted to know if there was something that she had done to offend him.

One of Jesus' main reasons for living on earth was to teach forgiveness, but that was not going to be easy for her to do. Marcus had wronged her without an explanation. He had lied to her and claimed to be supportive. Their relationship was what all her dreams had been made of and they hadn't even gotten intimate yet.

It was one thing to lose a church, but it was another thing to lose the trust of the man she hoped to call her husband. She went back into all her texts and the comments he sent during their relationship, but there were no clues. He was really good at what he did. It seemed like he had no conscience about it either. She had truly gone from the love of his life to his arch enemy. His evil was as swift as a thief in the night.

She was scheduled to give her last speech that morning to the church. Everyone had already heard about what happened, and she knew that the rumors had gotten out of control. She didn't even want to know what people were saying about her.

Her favorite emerald brooch was pinned on her black hat. She wore a black suit with a silver outline on the lapel. Her shoes were also silver and had a lower heel so she could be more comfortable.

The drive over to the church seemed longer than usual. She mourned at the fact that she would never make that trip again.

Arriving later than the start of service, she parked her car toward the back of the parking lot. She got ready to face all the stares and people shaking their heads out of pity.

A few people turned their heads toward her in the

parking lot, but no one tried to get eye contact.

Staci arrived inside the church from the choir stand. She walked down to the first row, where the sopranos sat. She found Martha and sat next to her. Staci felt the most warmth she had experienced in a long time when Martha clutched her shoulder. It was a simple gesture, but she could tell it was genuine.

Directly following announcements, Deacon Jameson approached the podium below the pulpit. He wiped his forehead with a cloth.

"Good afternoon, church!"

"Good afternoon," the churched echoed.

There was an obvious hint of tension in their air. Women clutched their children and men held their wives closer to them.

"So, we're going to have a speaker give you all a short presentation, and then we'll be on our way."

Staci made her way to the podium and collected herself before she spoke so she wouldn't start off in tears.

"Church, I come to you today to ask for your prayer. I ask you to forgive me for what I have done and for what I may not have done. I am stepping down today as your pastor. I will no longer be of service to the wonderful people of Center of Praise. After much discussion of possibilities, we have decided that it is best for me to move on from this great church. I will still be praising along with you. As you know, God will still be by my side. I will not be leaving the grand old Church of God in Christ any time soon. I believe that our doctrine is still right and God is still blessing those that live a saved and sanctified life in the Holy Spirit. I may not be in the building, but I hope you will continue to treasure all the wonderful memories we have shared. I love all of you, and to God be the glory forever and ever. Amen."

She turned her back to the crowd so she wouldn't have to face the tears and anguish left behind. Several people had covered their mouths, and a couple men shed a tear. The deacons kept their eyes elsewhere, and Marcus pretended to be engrossed in his Bible.

Martha stood to hug her, as did the rest of the choir. Todd jumped off his organ seat with tears in his eyes and said that she was the best pastor he had ever had the opportunity of serving under.

The youth department cried like someone had just passed away. Small children turned to their parents to ask what had happened. Once their mothers whispered that Pastor Bernard was leaving, they lowered their heads. One eight-year-old looked for the comfort of his mother and hugged her.

Staci grabbed her purse and Bible and left out the same way she came. Martha followed behind her.

"Pastor, this isn't the end. We can appeal to Abernathy."

"Abernathy won't be any good. He knows me, but he's going to trust those that have served in this church the longest. I've basically made him look like a fool and also ruined it for other women."

"That's not true! Those were all lies!"

"Martha, God will bless me again. I just have to trust him."

Staci dipped into her car and removed her hat. She exchanged her heels for slip-on sneakers and draped her suit jacket on the passenger seat.

She backed away from Martha, who was standing there trying not to shed a tear.

Staci didn't cry on her way back home. She felt a

sense of freedom. For the first time in a long time, no one would be depending on her. She would be able to get some cleaning and reading done. There were lots of things to help her parents out with around their house.

However, she was going to have to get a job soon to support herself. With a doctorate degree, she would be overqualified for most jobs, but she promised to humble herself to find something that would pay her rent.

Staci blocked Marcus' number on her phone and canceled all her social media accounts. The only number she kept unblocked was Martha's. Her former right-hand woman had been the most emotionally supportive during the week.

During the following few days, Staci did a job search. She hadn't told her parents what happened yet, but she was sure they would get the news.

For someone that had spent most of their time in school preparing to be a minister, she didn't feel prepared for any occupation outside of church. She looked at housekeeping positions, retail, driving for the city, and even a dishwasher at a local restaurant. Within a few hours of searching, Staci was beginning to feel defeated. Her rent was not cheap, and she had only saved up enough money to carry her through the next three months.

Staci went on the website of the university where she had earned her doctorate and saw that they were looking for an administrative assistant. It would be a hefty salary cut, but she filled the application out and hoped for the best.

Once she hit send, she heard her phone ring from the living room.

"Hello?" Staci said.

"Hi, Pastor. I don't care what anyone says. I'm still calling you that and you can't stop me. How's everything been?"

"Everything is okay. I just filled out an application to be an administrative assistant."

"Administrative assistant? You aren't interested in starting another church?"

"I can't even think about all that right now. It might be a possibility one day, but I don't think I'm ready to take that on at this moment."

"I think you're giving up too easily. How much will an administrative assistant pay?"

"Not enough to keep this apartment. I might have to move in with my parents and commute. I applied to my old program, where I got my doctorate. I'm also searching for teaching positions at a community college, but I haven't seen any pop up yet."

"Look, if need be and you find a job closer in, I don't mind you staying with us."

"No, Martha. I'll be fine. I promise."

"Todd and I wanted to take you out to dinner this week, if you were available. It's okay if it's too soon."

"I think I'll be ready by this week. Thank you, Martha."

❖

That Sunday, Staci was still trying to find a church to attend. She didn't want to go anywhere close to Watts, but she was hopeful she would find another COGIC church in the area. It scared her that her name had been run into the ground so much that any church she attended would know who she was. She wouldn't be welcome into the pulpit or barely welcome in the back row.

While searching online for nearby Pentecostal churches, Martha texted her that Marcus was going to be installed as pastor that day.

Well, congratulations, Staci texted back.

She had been able to successfully remove herself from any dealings with the church, so much so that she had forgotten that Center of Praise still hadn't gotten an official pastor.

She was genuinely glad that they had someone to take over that they knew.

I'm sickened but I'll send you updates on what happens.

Staci chose to go to a small, storefront Pentecostal church next to a gas station. Most COGIC churches were well connected and all knew each other but she had never heard of this one.

It was pastored by an eighty-year old man and his sixty-year old son. The church was small and they only had about eight members. Staci was elated when she arrived. The church members were all too old to be interested in social media and, luckily, had never heard of her.

They welcomed her with open arms and, once they heard that she had worked as an evangelist, wanted her to say a few words.

Staci even dressed more relaxed this time around. She wore a simple floral print dress and had her hair in a bun.

The pastor thanked her for joining their service and asked if she could come back.

She shook his hand and said she would definitely

be interested in coming back.

A sudden wave of emotion overcame her when the small choir began to sing. She missed her choir, praise dancers, and even Mother Earnestine screaming in a frenzy from her seat in the front. She missed the deacons dancing through the aisles and even the cooing babies she heard every time she spoke into the mic.

This church was quiet. It wasn't her church, but it would have to be home for now until God called her to another place of worship.

After benediction, Staci checked her phone. Martha had started a group chat with her and Todd to share what was happening during the installation service.

I can't believe this. He is acting like they're crowning him as king.

Martha sent a picture of Marcus being given a new

bible with a wide grin on his face. He had on an expensive suit that Staci recognized as the same one Marcus had eyed in Beverly Hills last time they took a trip there.

He just makes me sick. I'm not staying any longer but I have to convince my department that we can go elsewhere. I'd hate for us all to break up.

Oh, and he's got new rules! Todd interjected. **He wants musicians to only play during the choir selections and his sermon. He says playing during any other time, is disruptive.**

What? Staci gasped.

She shook her head and let them continue to alert her through the afternoon. She wished she hadn't deleted her social media so she could see what people were saying.

Do people look happy? Staci asked.

Absolutely not. A few walked out. I think the deacons are happy though. Mother Earnestine thinks he's going to bring back the old way they used to do things. That lady is a she-devil.

Well hopefully not too many of them leave. It's still a great church.

With a bad spirit, Martha answered. **It just doesn't feel right here.**

Staci closed out of her text messaging and got in her car. She feared that if she focused too much on what was going on, she would fall back into a deep depression. Things hadn't felt the same around her since she was ousted from Center of Praise.

Before driving off, she checked the emails from her phone. They were no longer flooded with dozens of texts from people from church. Instead, she saw two emails from jobs she had applied for that had rejected her. They were both assistant management positions in retail. She had hoped that her experience preaching and organizing multiple departments would lead to someone taking a chance on her.

Staci wanted to congratulate Marcus and unblocked his number.

Congratulations, sir.

He didn't text back. She planned on unblocking him once again.

It still hurt her that their relationship had dissolved, but she didn't want the church back anymore. Going back would be too difficult to do. She would have to gain the trust of everyone all over again.

Besides, she figured that the church would figure out Marcus' true intentions before it was too late. If he was stealing, he would be caught by one of the savvy deacons in no time. They used to be on her like white on rice, so she was happy that they would be in charge of bothering someone else for a change.

Thanks. He texted back.

She then blocked his number again and went about her day. There were so many more job applications to fill out before it got dark and she became too tired.

A prayer echoed through her heart as she drove home. She prayed for God to protect her, to keep the youth in perfect peace, and to reveal the truth to the church. All she wanted was the truth to come out to the public. Marcus could keep the church but, due to his actions, it would be a long time before anyone trusted her in the pulpit ever again. The scarlet letters of liar and thief might follow her to the grave.

❖

Staci finally got the courage to open her laptop and reactivate her account. Through Martha, she learned that she hadn't permanently deleted her account.

She took a deep breath and opened her church's social media page. The last time she went on, she was defending her sermon practices. This time around, she would probably see all kinds of gossip from people that had known her at Center of Praise. She braced herself to find hurtful comments from those that she had loved and trusted during her tenure.

Once the page appeared, she noticed that her image at the header at been removed. It used to feature her in a pink suit smiling. She had taken that photo with a professional photographer and had uploaded it about three weeks after she took over.

Now, it was a picture of Marcus smiling with his right hand clutching a bible. She saw that he had gold cufflinks and a gold crucifix that had been tucked into his shirt pocket. He wore a clerical collar as well. Staci could tell that he wanted to look as much like a man of God as possible. It was hilarious to her, but she hoped people could see right through them.

As she read the comments, she could tell that a lot of people couldn't.

There were so many members congratulating him and saying that they were happy to have him as pastor. He had outlined a few plans that he had for the church, such as incorporating a senior choir into the service once a month and for the church to raise money for his trip to Africa.

It hurt that people behaved as if everything was back to normal. It was as if she had never pastored. Staci remembered learning about Queen Hatshepsut in history. The Egyptian people were so angered that they had been subject to a female pharaoh, that any statues or writings that featured her were destroyed following her death. They wanted to make sure that their history was carefully curated to show that they had always been ruled by men.

While filling out applications and scrolling down the social media page, Staci called Martha.

"Hello?" Martha answered after one ring. "How's everything, Pastor?"

"I'm doing well. I'm just sitting here and I notice that they changed the church's social media page as quickly as they could. Center of Praise didn't waste any time. The people must really like him."

It had been almost one month since Staci had been at her old church. It was beginning to feel like she hadn't been there in years.

"No. That's just social media. I don't think people like him like that. You know, a lot of people were upset when you left. It wasn't the easiest transition."

"Well, this page says differently."

"For one, those people must have always had a problem with you or they're new. Two, we've lost over fifty members since he became pastor. A few of the people in my choir have moved on. A lot of people are jumping ship. The morale isn't the same as it used to be."

Staci was sad to hear that the church was losing members, but part of her was relieved that at least a few people were upset when she left.

"Wow, fifty? That's a lot of people."

"Yes, so don't take social media for the truth. He doesn't have a grip on the people like you did. His sermons are long and boring. He also has multiple offerings and has even hinted that the church should buy him a welcome gift. He said he needs God to bless him with a new car."

"That's a shame. You shouldn't be asking the

members for anything. Your job is to serve. He should be praying for people and preaching. If he can't do that, then maybe he doesn't need that position."

"See Pastor, that's why we need you! It's just not the same."

"Well, it would be nice to see how everything has changed, but I can't go back there."

"We have a livestream now. I know we were going to do that in the future, but Todd uses his phone with a tripod. Marcus wanted to put his sermons on social media."

"That's nice."

"Except that Todd isn't getting paid any more. He's already cut his salary for no reason and now wants him to be the technology person. You know how nice Todd is, so he went on and did it but I don't like that at all."

"Well, maybe I'll take a look at it soon."

With Martha on the phone, Staci looked at his personal social media page. They had never unfollowed each other.

On display was his new girlfriend. She was wearing the ring that he had proposed to her with, but it was on her other hand so she assumed he wasn't engaged. The woman was Latina and had long brown hair down to her waist. She looked a lot younger than him and wore revealing clothing. She didn't look First Lady material at all, but she looked happy with him.

He had several pictures where he took her on nice vacations, to expensive restaurants, and they had even gone on a private plane ride to New York. Marcus was living the life that he had only fantasized about with her. While she was with him, she was footing the bill or acknowledging all his excuses. Every time he "forgot" his wallet, she was right there to spot him. Her love had been so much greater than his and now that she saw how he paraded this new woman, it was obvious that was how it always was. Staci was beginning to wonder if Marcus had ever loved her at all.

He smiled a little bit harder with this woman, whose name was Marialena. The ring he gave her was just a small gift of appreciation. He draped her in everything luxury. She wondered how he could afford that much, even depending on the church. Because of her, the church had a sizable savings but it wouldn't have been enough to cover shopping sprees on Rodeo Drive.

"So, I see he has new woman?" Staci said.

"Yeah. I saw her. She absolutely looks like she's in it for the prestige. I don't even think she grew up Christian. I think she was Catholic. Anyway, she looks bored in the front pew. She always has her nose up in the air when we pass by her. She's even asked if we could play softer music, such as hymns; she says that we 'do too much' and she isn't used to it. So, Marcus has shut a lot of stuff out. He even stopped people from shouting too much. I heard from someone that he said he wants Center of Praise to turn into a more 'dignified' church. It's crazy."

Staci thought about how everything she built was crumbling right in front of her. Center of Praise took blood, sweat, and tears to get to where it was. Marcus was trying to tear down everything she had put in place to prove a point.

"I really wish you could come back. It just makes my heart so sad," Martha sighed.

"Well, I don't know about coming back, but maybe this isn't the end."

"What are you saying? You're going to start again?"

"Well, I don't know. Starting a church is a big deal.

It's not easy to get members and encourage them to actually join. It takes money, it takes networking, it takes capital. It's a lot."

"It's something that I know you can do, Pastor. 'I can do all things through Christ which strengthens me.'"

Staci had heard that quote repeatedly since she was a child but, this time, it pulled at her heartstrings more than it ever had before. A few tears fell from her face and dripped onto her neck. Images of her preaching and the pride her parents had overwhelmed her.

"Are you okay?" Martha asked.

"I'm fine. I just hadn't thought about that verse in a while."

"It's a beautiful verse. It needed to be said. You're doubting yourself. You're letting that man take away what you worked so hard for. Just because Center of Praise is not your building anymore doesn't mean that it isn't your congregation. Good people follow good pastors. You had your mind set on that church. You thought you'd be there forever. It didn't happen. This is the time to take back what's yours. He can have that church. I believe you were meant to be a pastor. You can't give up."

Staci sobbed for another few minutes and thanked Martha for the pep talk.

"Thank you, Martha. I'll think about it a little more carefully over the weekend."

"Stop filling out those job applications. God got you!"

Staci smiled and bid her goodbye.

She sank into her office chair and shut her laptop down. The sounds of the city calmed her. It was nice to finally focus in on the little things. Her mind was suddenly clear.

It was finally time for God to move.

❖

Staci arrived at her parents' home later that evening. She decided to make a surprise visit. Her mother hugged her so tightly, she felt like she could barely breathe.

"I missed you, too," Staci gasped.

Her father kissed her forehead and welcomed her into the dining room where they were just finishing up their dinner.

"Oh, Staci. I wish you would have told me. I would have made you something. Here, I have some more chicken, some collard greens. I can bake some more corn bread."

"No, Mother. It's fine. I'm not that hungry."

"Oh, hush. Let me feed you, gal!" her mother insisted.

"So, what brings you out this way?" her father asked, trying to scroll through his photo album on his phone.

"I know I haven't told either of you, but I was fired from Center of Praise. I'm sorry I kept it from you for so long."

"Fired?" her mother shrieked. "How? You just got that position. They can't do that. Only Abernathy…"

"Abernathy approved their charter from 1975 that said they are one of the few COGIC churches that is allowed to vote a pastor out with their deacon board. They accused me of so much stuff. They said I was stealing. They claimed I had purchased a bunch of luxury items on their dime. They basically called me a liar to my face. I had no fair counsel."

Her father lowered his eyes as if in deep thought and clasped his hands together in his lap. "Baby girl, they'll do that to you. You're a woman and you took over a man's church. When people have been in a church a long time and are used to one way, they'll do anything to get you out of there. I mean anything. I know they're a lie because I didn't raise no liar or no thief. They're basically talking about me. I wish you would have told me. I would have given those devils a piece of my mind."

Her father's voice rose and fell, like he was in belting an angry song.

"Staci," her mother muttered. "I was afraid that this would happen. There's always a risk involved when you inherit someone else's church. Those old people just wanted things to stay the same and they thought they would get that with a male. A lot of folk are still stuck on the old way and don't believe a woman is supposed to lead."

"And that's what he said. During my last meeting with them, Marcus mentioned that scripture where it says a woman should not lead men."

"Yeah, I've heard of that scripture," her father groaned. "It wasn't said by Jesus. It was written by one of his apostles. Jesus never said out of his mouth that a woman shouldn't lead. Also, I believe that God can use any mouthpiece to spread his word. If you don't praise him, the bible says that the rocks will."

Staci leaned on her father's shoulder. Although he was older and wasn't as strong as he used to be, leaning on his shoulder felt more sturdy than a rock.

"I was afraid you two would be so disappointed in me. I was embarrassed and that's why I waited so long to tell you."

"Staci, that's how that COGIC can go sometimes. You have never embarrassed me in your life. I'm so proud that I am the father of one of the most prolific female pastors this state, and maybe this country has ever seen. People still tell me how the videos they found of you online helped them. Your books are still being sold, too."

"I'm still looking for a job to support me, though. A real job."

"A job other than pastoring? No, baby. You were meant to be the pastor of a church," her father insisted. "Don't let the devil discourage you. He wants you to quit. He's laughing right now because you feel defeated. You know how you can stomp that devil? Take your ministry back. Don't be embarrassed. Not everybody believed those lies they spread about you."

"Believe me, Staci. The right people will be there for you. You always told me how the director of your youth department and your organist were always and still are in your corner. So you got people."

"So what should I do? I mean, I don't have a building. I don't have anything."

"You have your house right now, right?"

"Yes."

"Start there. Start with what you have. A building will come. You can't think about all that right now. Think about how you'll draw the people in."

Staci asked her parents if she could borrow a few sheets of paper. Her mother raced upstairs and brought down several blank notebooks. "Here, I've got plenty of paper. Let's think about this."

Ideas about how she would get the word out and when her services would start were outlined first. It felt odd to start a church from scratch. Most small churches closed down because they couldn't maintain a steady membership. Her heart was pounding with each bullet point she wrote down.

"Staci, when the Lord ordains a shepherd, the sheep have no choice but to follow. That's how it was designed. Take your staff and lead." Her father's words echoed through the house. She had never seen her father look at her with such seriousness before. It reminded her of when she used to get in trouble as a teenager.

She nodded with happy tears in her eyes this time. Then, she took her phone out of her purse.

Martha, I have a few ideas written down. I want you to see how all this sounds.

Chapter 9

She Has Risen

It was an ordinary Sunday morning with clear skies and the chipper barking of dogs echoing in the alleys behind her home. Staci made a cup of coffee, some toast, and added cheese to her scrambled eggs. She hadn't felt a true sense of calm in a long time. He head was clear and her conversation with her parents had increased her motivation.

She opened her laptop to take a look at the pages of notes she had taken. She had developed an entire map of the departments she wanted to have, who would be in charge of what, and where she hoped to find a building.

There hadn't been any definite plans to start

Sunday morning service at her home yet, but she was thinking that she would be ready to go in about three months. Her father and Martha encouraged her to just open the doors, let the people come in, and start from there. Staci wanted to work more carefully because losing her church the last time had caused her to have anxiety.

Staci, who had been dressing more casual lately, took a white blouse out of her closet and a blue pencil skirt. She had recently bought some elegant blue pumps and a purse to match. Although the people at the small church she had been attending weren't interested in fashion, she loved how dressing up improved her mood.

Todd texted her just as she was about to hop in the shower.

Hello, Staci. I was just thinking about you. I was wondering where you were headed to church today.

Todd had been texting her more often lately.

Initially, it was an annoyance but they were becoming good friends. She was beginning to feel the same friendly intimacy that she had with Martha.

I've been attending this small one near Crenshaw for now. I was going to go there this morning. You should come by.

I was wondering if you could come out to family and friends' day at Center of Praise. You don't have to come on time. We were having an afternoon service.

Martha had removed herself from Center of Praise so much that it was if she would be attending an entirely new church. She knew it wouldn't feel the same, but God's house was God's house.

I totally understand if you don't want to go but we've lost like one hundred members or more. A few of the deacons got sick. Bishop Jameson had a stroke last week actually. I forgot to tell you. It's not the same.

Last Sunday, only seventy people showed up.

So, you're saying it won't be as awkward? Staci texted back.

There's a lot of new members you probably don't know. However, that doesn't mean Marcus isn't acting like a big shot. You'd think he was the next TD Jakes. He keeps having these extra services so we can invite people. I just wanted you to see how far the church has fallen since you left.

Staci wasn't necessarily interested in watching the collapse of her old church, but she did want to see Todd on the organ again. He played exceptionally well and had a lovely singing voice. Everyone in the choir used to tease him and say that he knew how to make the organ "talk."

Ok, I'll think about it. I'll still go to my church. What time does the afternoon service start?

3:30

❖

When she opened the doors to the church from the entrance for non-ministry, one of the usher's eyes widened like a small child seeing their mother. She was hugged and kissed so many times, Staci could tell she smelled like several types of perfume and cologne at once.

Marcus was in the middle of having remarks before the choir planned to sing again. He saw her and quickly averted his eyes.

"You know, church. There will always be people out there that don't believe in you. People will be jealous of your success, but you go to keep praying! Church, can I get an Amen?"

He wiped his forehead and tried his best to look in

every direction but Staci. She knew it would be hard for him to do this because the church was not as full as it used to be.

"It really is a shame when folks want to watch your downfall!"

Staci saw Todd roll his eyes and continue to play a soft hymn to not respond to the power that Marcus was trying to put behind his speech.

Suddenly, Staci saw Marcus begin panting as if he was losing his breath. He hadn't even started preaching, but seemed oddly tired for someone that had stood up a few minutes ago.

Staci watched Marcus look around him, clutch the pulpit and say, "I can't catch my…"

He lost his balance and fell in the pulpit like a rag doll. The deacons, ministers, and other men in the audience tried to wake him up. Staci rushed toward the pulpit as well. Todd was already on the phone with 911.

The drummer, who knew CPR, tried to press into Marcus' chest and breathe into him. He wasn't responding. Staci asked if anyone could splash cold water on his face because she assumed he just fainted.

Then someone screamed, "He has no pulse! I think his heart stopped beating! Jesus!"

His girlfriend, Marialena, screamed so loud, the echo reverberated through the church for several more seconds once she fell to the ground as if in pain.

The ambulance rushed to the scene within eight minutes of being called.

One of the emergency responders had a gurney that he was pushing in front of him. One of the young men from the ambulance checked his pulse and then asked for the machine needed to restart his heart. They kept trying. The church was silent while they worked. Even the babies closed their mouths.

The man working on Marcus shook his head and sighed.

"I'm sorry. He's gone."

"Gone!" Deacon Brown cried.

The emergency responders placed his body on a gurney and then covered it with a sheet.

Staci held onto Martha, who had no tears in her eyes. Staci let the tears flow, and Todd came around to offer her his suit pocket square. She took it and then leaned into him. He wrapped his arms around her and told her that it was okay.

The three of them went outside. The entire church

was in tears, and almost everyone was on their phones, trying to tell somebody else what just happened. Marialena disappeared in his car and, apparently, was never heard from again.

"He's gone. Just like that," Staci sighed. "Wow."

"The bible says touch not my anointed and do my prophet no harm. Why do you think Todd and I worked so hard to protect you, Pastor?"

Staci teary eyes dried up in seconds.

"It's time for you to lead. This is the time. Not in three months, not in two weeks. Now."

"And I'll support you in any way I can. I'm your musician," Todd said cheerfully.

"And I'm your youth director, choir director, praise team, or whatever you want me to be."

Staci nodded. "It's time."

❖

City of Miracles Church of God in Christ opened its doors one week later in her home. The first day had twenty-five people. Todd had to go out and buy more chairs, just to make sure everyone had somewhere to sit.

Bishop Abernathy approved their charter and was satisfied that another church was growing under her leadership.

Todd, Martha, and Staci eventually put their money together to put a down payment on a mid-size building in South Los Angeles.

It would be able to seat at least one hundred people.

Within three weeks of the church opening, word

had spread so quickly that Staci was a pastor again, they had almost reached capacity and had to talk to contractors about how to build a balcony. Staci was also going to have to figure out how to have more than one service throughout the day to accommodate so many people.

Her former members from Center of Praise all heard about City of Miracles, either online or through word of mouth. Many of those she thought had been glad to see her go were elated that she had begun a new church.

Her praise dancers, her youth choir, and the musicians from Center of Praise had followed her.

Staci heard that the only people left at Center of Praise were the remaining deacons. Within a year, they would decide to lock the church's doors for good and disperse.

After a year of being open, City of Miracles had raised enough money to build a new church building with a steeple and beautiful stained glass windows. It would have a balcony, choir stand, classrooms, a dining hall, and even a daycare center.

As promised, Staci loved how Todd was right by her side every step of the way. He made decisions that made sense and was just as frugal as she was.

The things that made him seem dorky before were now excellent qualities. He was a serious and honest businessman. Their friendly lunches began to get more serious. He was funny, a great storyteller, and talented.

"It seems like you and Todd have something in common, huh?" Martha teased one day.

"We're talking. We're friends," Staci said, trying to hide her wide and giddy smile.

❖

On the church's first anniversary service, the choir had rocked the house. There were more members at City of Miracles than Center of Praise had ever seen. The praise dancers were the delight of everyone, and her youth numbers skyrocketed. City of Miracles was the hottest church to attend in town. Her reach on social media was unprecedented. Pastors that had been popular for years with an even larger membership had been trying to get ahold of her social media team.

Staci stood up to speak to her delighted audience once it was her time to thank everyone for a wonderful service. They had gifted her with a new purple suit, and each department raised money to support the church's many outreach programs.

"Church, I just want to say I love you!"

"We love you, Pastor Staci!"

Staci liked how her first name sounded. It was

becoming more popular with younger pastors to ditch their last name.

"I just wanted to thank all of you for supporting me thus far. I know it's been a long road but for those that have stuck by me, thank you. Thank you with the love of Jesus Christ. I have no one to thank but my God. He's been so good to me. This truly is the greatest congregation in the world. City of Miracles, I owe it to you!"

The membership stood and clapped in unison. A few shook their tambourines in the air and started a congregational song.

> *God's got a way*
> *That you can't go under*
> *God's got a way*
> *That you can't go over*
> *God's got a way that you can't go 'round it*
> *You must come in at the door!*

Directly following the song, Staci watched Todd suddenly stand up from his organ. He began to walk toward her. She saw that Martha was already beaming and move her body forward, as if in expectation of something to come.

Todd grabbed the mic from the pulpit and took her hand to lead her down to floor level.

"What's going on, Todd?"

Todd got down on one knee and took out a ring box. It featured a beautiful sapphire surrounded by diamonds. It looked like the ring that Princess Diana wore when she married Prince Charles.

"Todd?"

"Staci Evangline Bernard. Will you marry me?"

The crowd erupted with praises toward the couple.

"Yes. Yes I will, Todd."

Staci couldn't hold back her tears, and Todd stood to hold Staci in his arms as tightly as he could.

"I love you, Staci. I always loved you. I believe in you," Todd whispered in her ear.

"I love you, Todd. It's so amazing that the Lord may not be there when you want him…"

"But he's right on time," Todd answered.

"Right on time, Todd. Right on time."

The End

Social Media:

Instagram: @AuthorDMLavigne

Facebook: Destiny Writes (@Destiny.Writes90)

To submit a manuscript to be

considered, email us at

submissions@majorkeypublishing.com

Be sure to LIKE our Major Key
Publishing page on Facebook!